WHAT IS ADAM BLESSING LIKE?

Dorothy: "He's *terrific.*"

Charity: "He's *horrible.*"

Eloise: "He's *irresistible.*"

Shirley: "He's *a nut.*"

Ethel: "He's *divine.*"

Vera: "He's *revolting.*"

Ada: "He's *killing me.*"

The Damnation
of Adam Blessing

Vin Packer

PROLOGUE BOOKS

F+W Media, Inc.

Published in electronic format by
PROLOGUE BOOKS
an imprint of F+W Media, Inc.
10151 Carver Road
Blue Ash, Ohio 45242
www.prologuebooks.com

eISBN 10: 1-4405-3716-X
eISBN 13: 978-1-4405-3716-5

POD ISBN 10: 1-4405-5607-5
POD ISBN 13: 978-1-4405-5607-4

This work has been previously published in print format by:
Gold Medal Books / Fawcett Publications, Inc., Greenwich, CT.

PART ONE

1

"I dreamed again last night that I was Billy."
FROM ADAM BLESSING'S JOURNAL

Mrs. Auerbach was drunk again.

In the five years that Adam Blessing had worked for her, he had seen her drunk only once or twice a week. Things were getting worse lately; she was seldom sober. This Saturday afternoon in early May was her sixth consecutive day on the bottle. As usual she arrived at The Autograph Mart a moment or so before closing.

Adam had been calling her since noon about the customer for "The Lucy Baker Album."

"Where the customer is, Adam?" she asked, huffing and puffing her way across the floor of the basement shop.

Her habit was to eat a whole roll of peppermint life savers as she made her way from her apartment on Second Avenue and Fifty-seventh Street. It was a distance of three city blocks in a straight line, as straight as Mrs. Auerbach could manage.

"The customer," he said flatly, "is gone! He was in three times last week, twice this week. He won't be back."

"Goodt! He doesn't want it enough! I don't want to sell it to him anyway! That is a law, Adam!"

"Yes, ma'am," said Adam. "Why don't we just make it a law that we don't sell anything to anyone?"

The old woman ignored the sarcasm. With considerable effort she lowered herself to the folding chair before the card table which was her desk. She blew at some dust on top of old papers there. "Collectors do not interest me, Adam." She pulled a bottle of rum out of the wire wastebasket under the card table, and set it in front of her. "A customer must love what he buys from me, enough to come back a hundred times if he has to! To collectors I don't sell! Adam, they are worse than parasites, these collectors! They are saprophytes, who off the dead live!" She unscrewed the cap of the rum bottle. "Well, that collector is not going to live off Lucy Baker!" she said, and she punctuated it with a long swallow of rum.

Adam said, "We aren't going to live off her either."

Mrs. Auerbach was fat and in her late sixties. She always wore sweaters and skirts, even in the hot months, and silk stockings with ankle socks over them, and low black oxfords which were always polished. Her garters never reached above her knees. They were rolled to a stop an inch below her skirt. Her hair was a peculiar orange shade from the self-administered rinses. She wore it long, past her shoulder blades, and when she thought about it, she tied it in place with a piece of rough, brown wrapping cord. Today, she had not thought about it. She kept blowing at it from the sides of her wrinkled mouth, trying to keep it out of her eyes. Often when Adam was confronted with her dishevelment, he was reminded of the way she never dotted her *i*'s or crossed her *t*'s—bald proof of her absent-minded carelessness.

"So!" she said, setting the bottle back on the card table with a thud. "The City wins, no, Adam?"

Adam knew it was starting—another of Mrs. Auerbach's harangues against the city of New York. They were going to tear down the apartment house where she had lived for over thirty years. Already she was the only tenant remaining in the building; the gas and electricity had been turned off a week ago. Adam knew this was one of the reasons she was drinking so heavily lately. He sneaked a look at his wrist watch. Five past five. His date with Dorothy Schackleford was for six-fifteen at the Roosevelt Hotel.

"Mrs. Auerbach—" he tried, but she waved his words away with her pudgy hand.

She said: "I saw you. You are rushing so much all the time! All the time watching your clock, ah, Adam?

Hasn't that been the trouble with the business, your rushing? In this business, no one rushes and makes one dime! You rush like the City rushes!"

"You never even arrive here until five o'clock, Mrs. Auerbach. Don't forget that."

"I once thought I would make you my beneficiary. You are young, you could carry on the business, but no! You rush too much! I leave the whole shooting match to the Universal Committee on Conversation!"

"Conservation!" Adam corrected her.

It was her favorite threat, to cut him out of her will. Adam wondered if she even had a will. It was a five o'clock threat, when she wanted him to sit and drink rum with her, and listen to her curse Commercialism, Collectors, Waste, Progress and the City. Her mood could just as easily swing, in a matter of minutes. Then she would offer Adam the autograph album which had belonged to Goethe's son, or she would announce to Adam that she was planning to adopt him legally as her son and heir, or she would inform him that it was the U.C.C. she was cutting from her will, because they were doing nothing about topsoil research. She was magniloquent in both moods, either offering Adam the world, or offering to pull it out from under him. There was no in-between, such as an offer of an extra five-dollar raise. Adam was still making the measly seventy-five dollars a week he had been earning for the past two years.

"Everything to the Universal Committee on Conservation!" she babbled on. "They want to preserve, Adam! You don't want to preserve! What do you care if some unprincipled saprophyte walks in to buy 'The Lucy Baker Album?' You would sell it in a blink of the eye!"

Adam sighed and walked across to his desk, starting to clear away the day's work. He said, "You know nothing about the man who wanted to buy that album."

"Where he is? Not here. Ah? He wants to buy, but he has no time to wait! I would sell it to him under no circumstances!"

"You're stubborn," said Adam. "Just stubborn!"

"What?"

"Nothing."

"Yah, nothing! I heard you under your breath! You

and the City! Same birds!" She took another swallow of rum. " 'Remember well and bear in mind, that a true friend is hard to find.' "

It was a verse from "The Lucy Baker Album."

"So is a good living hard to find," said Adam.

"Quit the whole shooting match if you don't like it! Anyway, you're fired! I fired you a hundred times, and you don't get it through your head!"

"All we sell any more," Adam said, "is autographs. We haven't sold an autograph album in seven months!"

"Sell all the autographs you want to," said Mrs. Auerbach, holding the rum bottle to the light to see its level. "Who cares for an old slip of paper with Button Gwinnett scrawled on it? Ah? Yah, worth money, but who cares for it? And all the other signers of your Declaration to Independence! Some independence when the City comes to wreck your home!"

" 'The Lucy Baker Album' could have paid for a whole remodeling job here," Adam grumbled.

Mrs. Auerbach chuckled. "I hate to sell the albums, Adam. The autograph books—there's where my heart is. The *Stammbuchs,* with all their sweet sentiments! There's the heart in this business, and you would sell it! Sell Button Gwinnett's *schlimm* signature, but leave me my heart!"

"Never mind," said Adam. "Sunday I'll look in the *Times* for something. Some other work!"

Mrs. Auerbach did not raise her eyes from the rum bottle. She had heard that before. She knew how Adam loved The Mart. For Adam too, the autograph books were the most interesting part of the business. He loved to study the handwriting of the people who wrote in them; handwriting analysis had become his hobby. He enjoyed imagining the friendships, love affairs, and family relationships, and more than often he could pick out the most sinister dips and loops written in some of the saccharine and homely verses; as well as the contrary in some of the most dull and proper entries. Adam had never had a knack for making friends; love was a word which still sounded clumsy and joyless on his tongue. He had been raised in the Cayuga County Orphans' Home, in upstate New York, and the closest he had ever come to having a family was his hero-worship of a very wealthy man in the city. But this same man had a son of his own with whom Adam had never succeeded in getting along; the son, in fact, had been the blight of Adam's young years, always teasing him and showing him up. Adam had come away from upstate New York with a fierce embarrassment at having been an orphan. Often, with strangers, he invented a family; more than often he pretended to be the son of that rich man, using this masquerade only in the very unimportant moments—riding on a train or a bus, or having a drink beside someone in a bar. It was a little peculiarity of Adam's, and he did it without thinking, as though it were a perfectly normal thing to do. Usually he kept his own name, but there had been times when he went the limit, and said his name was Billy Bollin.

Mrs. Auerbach was the only person with whom he had ever discussed his past in detail, and honestly. She was old and warm and sentimental, in her better moments, and, he supposed, slightly daffy as well, but Adam could talk to her. When he had first come to New York and taken this job with her at The Mart, they had spent many long hours talking together. Mrs. Auerbach could carry on forever over a rum bottle, but never once had she told Adam anything about her past.

At twenty-four, Adam Blessing was a little under six feet, with strong muscles he had worked hard to develop, a pleasant manner, and a good appearance—which had also involved work. As a youngster he had been very fat, and far from neat; he had been slow in school, and the dolt of his classmates. The course he had run since leaving Auburn, New York had not been an easy one; it had been all uphill. He had enrolled in numerous adult education classes given in high schools around the city. He had taken speech and shorthand, a semester of German, art appreciation, music appreciation, ballroom dancing, economics, a course in business management and one in personality. He was not as shy as he used to be, and he was meticulous about combing his white-blond hair and parting it in a somewhat old-fashioned way on the

far left side. He kept himself scrubbed clean, nails
clipped, clothes pressed and immaculate. His face was
not overly-endowed by Nature with perfect features, but
he had a good nose and excellent teeth, which com-
pensated for lips that were on the small side, and eyes
that were a dull, yellowish brown, Adam could easily be
taken for a school teacher, a seminary student, a teller
in a bank; or for exactly what he was—Mrs. Auerbach's
clerk.

This outward appearance of mild-mannered intro-
version was misleading. Adam Blessing was ambitious.
His ambitions kept him awake nights, sent him on long
walks through dawn-deserted city streets, and kept him
writing letter after letter after letter to manufacturers,
corporations, agencies and any number of private enter-
prises. He was a world of ideas without an axis on which
to revolve. When his letters received any replies at all,
they were simply polite acknowledgments; more frequent-
ly they were ignored. Adam imagined that they were
probably laughed at, and often, just after he mailed one
of his letters, his cheeks would smart with frustration
and humiliation as he imagined the letter arriving, and
being ridiculed. His ideas for a way to improve paper
clips, for children's games, for advertising copy, for
packaging pickles and olives in lighter containers, for
promoting books and for publishing more readable newspapers—all of Adam's ideas were unrealized. He needed
money; even ideas for making money cost money. That
fact was his dead end.

Waking and sleeping, he dreamed of having money, but
in those moments of stark reality when he was face to
face with the glaring light of truth, he became resigned
and somewhat bitter. He was Adam Blessing, no matter if
he could see his reflection only hazily in the mirror behind the bar, no matter if the stranger beside him did put
his beer down, shake his hand and say: "Glad to know
you, Mr. Bollin."

After he had piled his correspondence neatly and rolled
down the top of his desk, he glanced across at Mrs. Auerbach. She was humming a waltz. Some of the rum had
dribbled down the front of her red sweater from the sides

of her mouth, and her legs were spread in a careless fashion, so that Adam could see up to the long pink silk bloomers she wore; could see the jelly-fat-flabby thighs. He had seen her that way too many times to figure, but each time he was reminded of the only glimpse of his own mother which his memory retained. He was not even certain of how old he was, but he must have been very young, for it was some time before he had been taken to the Home. He was in a kitchen with her. She had been washing clothes at the sink on a hot day, and she had plopped herself down on a straight-backed wooden chair, in the same posture as Mrs. Auerbach's now. He had not been too young to feel a certain shame at being able to see up her skirt. She was not fat like Mrs. Auerbach. Adam could not remember her face. But he did remember something she said to him. Her tone was sarcastic. Adam liked to think that it was a sarcasm striped with a certain disappointment about something Adam had nothing to do with, but he could not be positive of that. He only knew for sure that she had looked at him and said, "And a lot *you* care!"

That was the only memory Adam had of a parent.

Mrs. Auerbach's mood had swung now. She was telling Adam that she was leaving him everything when she passed on. Adam was convinced she would leave it to dogs and cats, the Committee on Conservation, or perhaps some imaginary committee of her own, to fight the city of New York. He sometimes wondered what happened to an old woman's money when she had no beneficiary; but whatever did happen, and whoever did take over the business, Adam was sure he would be asked to stay on. In addition, he was sure his position would be a more important one. He knew as much about the stock at The Mart as Mrs. Auerbach did, and he had hundreds of ideas for making the place a success. Mrs. Auerbach was simply not interested in the business any more, despite her occasional harangues to the contrary. Whoever took over the business—and even in Adam's dreams he discounted himself, for he knew the old woman and her crazy ways—the new owner would need Adam. It would be a matter of time. Adam would be given more responsibility and more money, and while he would probably not get rich, he would have enough, he was sure . . .

Drunk or sober, Mrs. Auerbach embraced strangeness with the unreasoning enthusiasm of the certifiable eccentric. Adam knew that she often picked through city litter baskets for strange souvenirs—an old box, a hat band—once, the wheel of a baby carriage. It had been reported to Adam, by other shopkeepers along Fifty-seventh Street, that she kept thousands of dollars in used sardine tins in her icebox; and Adam was very used to seeing the jar of pepper she carried at all times, to ward off thieves.

About Mr. Auerbach—whoever he was, and if he ever had been—Adam knew nothing. Mrs. Auerbach mentioned no relatives, except to say she had lived a lovely life and it was done with some years ago; that now she and Adam were both orphans.

He walked across and sat down at the card table with Mrs. Auerbach, waving away her offer of the rum bottle. It was now twenty minutes past five. Adam's date was with an airline reservations telephone clerk he had met in his personality class.

"Mrs. Auerbach, I have to go soon. Really."

She was paging through the familiar autograph book, her favorite.

"This is the great poet Goethe's son's autograph book, Adam."

"Yes, ma'am, I know that by now."

"Yes, ma'am, you know, don't you? It's yours, but you think I should put it back in the safe. You don't believe it's yours, no?" She cackled and drank more rum. "My apartment was mine. Thirty years, Adam, yah? I believed it was mine, but no! The City's it was—all these years. Did the City pay the rent once? No, but the City's it is!"

"I'm sorry about that Mrs. Auerbach, I really am."

"But you're a hurry. Rush and rush, Adam, is that you? Like the City, rush and rush to get me out."

"I have a date, Mrs. Auerbach."

"Yes, but wait, Adam." She placed her hand on Adam's wrist. "The law is, this is yours. Take it." She put the worn autograph book in his hands. "It was Goethe's son's book, Adam. Oh, money it could bring you, and not a little. But more, Adam. Sentiment. Roots. Let it be your *Stammbuch,* Adam. Roots, I can't give you, but this is the next best thing. Yah, Adam?"

"Thank you," said Adam. "I'll put it back in the safe."

She slapped her hand down on the book in his hand. "Nein! This time, take it with you! It is yours, Adam!"

Adam said, "Yes, and thank you again. I'll keep it here in the safe."

"Nein!"

Adam held the book in his hand, uncertain of his next step. In all his years of receiving this "gift" from Mrs. Auerbach, she had never stopped him from putting it back in the safe; neither of them, Adam always thought, had ever taken her gesture with any seriousness. The book was worth thousands; it was one of The Mart's most valuable pieces of stock.

" 'Hand to the patron the book, and hand it to friend and companion,' " Mrs. Auerbach recited. "I hope you will over and over read that, Adam. In Goethe's own handwriting."

Adam said, "This book is worth—"

"Money! Is that all you care for? Put it in your pocket and shut up your squealing and squeaking! I need some peace! You are like a collector with your money all the time! Put it in your pocket!"

Adam did as he was told.

"Go on, rush!" she said. "Shoo!"

"I could—help you home, Mrs. Auerbach."

Momentarily she regarded him coolly, letting his presumption hang in the silence. Adam had thought of walking her the few blocks to her apartment, then slipping back with the valuable book and locking it safely in The Mart. It was no good. "Since when did I need help home, Herr Blessing?"

He knew she was very angry.

"The law about 'The Lucy Baker Album stands!' " she announced, with a bang of the rum bottle on the table top for punctuation. "To that man who comes here for it, it is not for sale."

"Yes, ma'am."

"And there is filing piled up on your desk too!"

"I realize that, Mrs. Auerbach."

"Do you have correspondence on the Poe manuscript?"

"Yes, Mrs. Auerbach. I have it started."

"Go on! Next thing you'll want this overtime employees want, yah?"

"No," Adam said.

He kept the palm of his hand on his pocket where the album was. He knew he would keep it there all night, and that he would sleep with it under his pillow; not draw a free breath until it was back in The Mart on Monday. He could not even return it tomorrow, though he had a key. At 6:00 P.M. on Saturdays, Mrs. Auerbach's burglar alarm was wired to the keyhole, and centralized with the Palmer Protective Association. It was clocked that way until eight Monday morning.

"What are you waiting for, ah?" She sat erect now, with her plump legs crossed, the one dangling over the other, swinging—exposing her garter, her silk stockings, and her bright yellow ankle socks. As always, Adam could see his face in the shine on her shoes. He dismissed a crazy, sudden impulse to bend down and plant a kiss on that wild mop of orange hair.

As he turned, after saying good night, he heard her voice behind him snap: "Get in on time Monday morning, Herr Blessing!"

Outside, he climbed the winding stairs to Fifty-seventh Street. He sneaked a look at her, the naked electric light bulb dangling on a cord directly above her head, the bottle of rum tipped to her mouth, and her feet tapping energetically to what Adam guessed was probably another waltz.

2

"My youth was eaten away by Envy. Even in my sleeping dreams I imagined that I was Marshall Bollin's son. Once when I was nine he said to me, 'Adam, I'd be very proud if you were my boy.' . . . I wrote it down on a piece of paper and put 'M.C.

*Bollin' after it, the way you'd copy a piece of poetry
out of a book. I put the date at the top, and over
the date I wrote 'Spoken to Adam Blessing.' . . .*
FROM ADAM BLESSING'S JOURNAL

"You *are* Adam Blessing, aren't you?" the voice inquired. "Adam Blessing from Auburn, New York?"

For some slow seconds everything stopped, the way a slow-motion camera will grind to a halt on the pole-vaulter in mid-air, show him grimacing and dangling there, suspended in time.

Musak provided a harmonica rendition of "Tangerine."

At the table across from Adam in the Roosevelt Grill, the waiter was wiping up a spilled Manhattan.

Dorothy Schackleford, Adam's date, was holding out a souvenir for Adam, an ashtray she had stolen from Alfredo's in Rome.

The voice came like a sudden clap of black thunder on an ordinary and fair day . . . Adam had always known it would happen this way, when he least expected it; so that the shock was still curling through his body as he rose and faced Billy Bollin. . . . Time began again.

"Yes, it's Adam," reaching for Billy's outstretched hand. "Hello, Billy."

"Adam! Addie! My God, Addie!" Billy pounded him on the back.

"How are you, Billy?"

"I can't believe my eyes, Addie! God, Addie Blessing! Old Fatty Addie! Look at you!" he said, holding Adam back, "Why, you're as thin as—" hesitating, searching for a simile.

"As you are," said Adam.

"Yes!"

"Yes."

"Well, my God, Addie Blessing!"

Billy had not changed. He still stood taller than Adam, and there was the same tanned handsomeness about him, which offset his shock of bright red hair. His jade-colored eyes sparkled with the same arrogant confidence, and he wore the same sort of rich and casual clothes—a black and white shepherd's check jacket, coal-colored slacks, crisp white shirt, and a blue twill silk tie. He had dressed that way even as a young boy. Adam took it all in, right down to the gold cuff links with the simple soft-printed *B* embellishing their faces.

He introduced Billy to Dorothy Schackleford. He could tell by the crooked grin on his know-everything face that Billy had sized her up immediately. She was pretty but she was plain, and plainly impressed already by Billy Bollin. Her brown hair was fuzzy from a home permanent she had over-timed. There was a slight scorch mark on one of her white cotton gloves, resting atop her shiny black patent leather bag. Billy will patronize her, Adam thought, and Billy did.

"Oh," said Billy, "an ashtray from Alfredo's, ah? You've been to Rome!"

"Where I work we can go for practically nothing," said Dorothy. "I'm a clerk for Pan-Trans-America. I got this ashtray from Alfredo's for Adam, because he's given me some swell ones! The Sherry-Netherland, the Stork Club, the Twenty-One—all over, haven't you Adam? Where else, Adam?"

Adam blushed with embarrassment. "I don't remember."

"The El Morocco, that's another one! Gosh, I don't even know all the places. Adam's good at it, aren't you, Adam? I thought I'd die of fright while I was getting this into my bag, but I thought to myself: I've got to get one from Europe for Adam. Adam's never been, have you, Adam?"

Her round, red-cheeked face was glowing, and her nose was shining as well. Adam noticed for the first time that her lipstick was too purple, that she had shaped her lips into a vulgar cupid's bow.

Adam shook his head in reply to her remark, aware of the satisfaction the scene must be giving Billy. Here was Fatty Addie, thin now but not much different; grown-up now, but still tagging at the heels of the rich—collecting ashtrays from the restaurants of the rich, sneaking around and pocketing evidence that he had been to them. Adam imagined Billy entertaining some of his friends with the story of this moment—imagined him beginning: "When I knew Addie, he was a fat kid from the county Home; in a way you might say Addie and I grew up together . . . only, of course, I wasn't an orphan. My old man is Marshall Case Bollin; the good Lord knows whose Addie's is, or was—pause for a snide chuckle—"or if he had one!"

"Adam," Billy was saying now, "grew up with me. Didn't you, Addie?"

"You might say," Adam answered, "that we grew up together."

Billy regaled Dorothy Schackleford by telling her what a fat little boy Adam had been, how he was always eating or bawling or trailing after Billy's father. Dorothy giggled appreciatively, lighted one cigarette from the other before Adam could offer a light, and looked up admiringly at Billy in the manner of the female positive she had made a hit.

"But I've nearly forgotten my date!" said Billy suddenly.

Dorothy Schackleford was visibly disappointed at this announcement. Adam felt a wave of wild relief . . . until Billy added, "I'll go get her. She's in the back. We'll all have a round together!"

He pranced toward the rear of the room. Adam intended to announce to Dorothy that they would not go through with Billy's plan, but as he felt for his wallet to pay their bill, his hand brushed against the valuable *Stammbuch* given him an hour ago by Mrs. Auerbach. A crazy impulse captured him. He slid his wallet back in place and leaned forward, speaking in a low voice to Dorothy Schackleford.

"I am part owner of The Mart," he said quite clearly.

"Okay," she said, "I'm Brigitte Bardot."

"Listen to me, Dorothy, I'm serious. When he gets back I'm going to tell him I'm part owner of The Autograph Mart. It's practically true!"

"Adam, it isn't true. That old biddy pays you slave wages as it is!"

"Dorothy, won't you do me a favor?"

"I don't mind going along with a gag, Adam. I just don't want you to think it's 'practically true.' "

Adam said, "Listen, right here in my pocket," patting

his suit jacket for emphasis, "I have an album she gave me which is worth close to $50,000. She gave it to me tonight."

"Goethe's son's album?" she said sarcastically . . . Adam had not remembered having spoken before about Mrs. Auerbach's drunken offers of the album, forgotten by her, or simply reneged in her sober moments—Adam was never sure which.

"All right," he said, "but tonight she forced me to take it!"

"You'll put it back in stock Monday."

"Maybe I will. Maybe I won't." He sounded unconvincing even to himself.

"You'll put it back in stock, and that's as close as you'll ever come to that much money from her!"

"I'm her beneficiary, Dorothy."

"Like I said, Adam, I'm Brigitte Bardot!"

Adam glanced toward the back of the room nervously. Then in a more urgent tone he said, "I'm asking you to do me this favor. It's important to me!"

"All right, Adam! And you don't live at the Y either, I suppose. You live at the Waldorf Towers!"

"That's right," said Adam, "I don't live at the Y."

"My gosh, you're dead serious, aren't you?"

"Dead serious," said Adam.

Dorothy looked at him with a puzzled expression on her plain countenance. Adam wished he had never noticed the purple lipstick or the cupid's bow. He knew he was seeing her through Billy's eyes; seeing everything through Billy's eyes now, the way he used to. Dorothy Schackleford shrugged and stood up. "Before this circus begins," she said, "I'm going to use the sand box."

Whenever she said that, she put her arms up close to her shoulders, curling her fingers into her palms, imitating, Adam supposed, a cat on its hind legs. To frost the absurdity, she gave a mew, and whined: "Would Adam order pussy-cat another drinky-poo?"

Adam was just glad Billy was not witness to that moment.

Adam sat alone then, resigned to imminent embarrassment of some kind. For himself, he could carry it off, act the part—even produce the *Stammbuch*. Billy would believe him when he saw the *Stammbuch;* Billy knew what was and what was not worth money. Adam wished he was alone, wished he had had this dreaded encounter with Billy Bollin when he was by himself. With any other girl, Adam could have pretended he had given her the ashtrays from Those Restaurants because he *knew* it would impress her, and because he knew it was one way to get her into bed. His receiving the ashtray from Alfredo's could even have been crossed off as an act of going along with her naïveté, for the same reason . . . Except that Dorothy Schackleford was not the kind of girl one imagined a man panting after. She would embarrass him, that was all there was to it; she was the flaw in his pose. Adam remembered a time when he had embarrassed Dorothy Schackleford, before a gathering of *her* friends. He had gotten very drunk and he had criticized the presence of an imitation fireplace in one of her girlfriends' apartments; he had crowned the occasion by throwing up in the bathroom of the apartment. Dorothy Schackleford had told him she had never been so embarrassed in all her life. It had been their first date. She was really ashamed of him and angry. She had said she had not minded his getting sick so much as she had minded his attack on the fireplace. The fireplace, she had raged at him, had cost her girlfriend a good deal of money, and the fact that Adam could not appreciate a fine piece of furniture made her embarrassed. Her girlfriend would think Adam had been brought up in a barn, she said. He might just as well have criticized the Mettropolitan Museum for hanging an El Greco, as far as Dorothy Schackleford was concerned.

Embarrassment was an unpredictable enemy. It could react on individual conceits as personal and diversified as one's taste in underwear. Maybe, if Billy got to the table before Dorothy returned, Adam could give the impression she was just a girl who did typing for him occasionally, a spare-time job of hers, to earn a little extra money. Even as he thought it, he felt low, a feeling familiar to him from years back when Billy Bollin would make him react this same way. Yet he knew there was no way out; around Billy he was this sort of shabby person. In that way, Adam Blessing had not changed at all, and he had known it the instant he had heard Billy's voice call out his name.

Adam wondered what it was that would embarrass a Billy Bollin: perhaps that his fly had been open all through a Philharmonic concert; perhaps that he—but the next possibility remained unborn.

"Here we are, Addie!"

Certainly the almost-forgotten date would not embarrass Billy.

Adam stared at her as he stood up.

Billy said, "This is Charity Cadwallader."

Was that how it all began?

3

> *"More than anything in the world I wanted to be like Billy. I wanted to have what he had, and I believed that if I were ever to change places with him, I'd know better and wiser ways to enjoy his advantages. His father, for example—I would have been a good son to Marshall Bollin. I would have—but what's the use in mulling over the past! I must stop this constant mulling over of the past!*
>
> FROM ADAM BLESSING'S JOURNAL

Adam thought about her constantly. That Monday morning it was raining when he caught the crosstown bus. He had wrapped the *Stammbuch* in a brown paper bag and placed it under his coat to keep it dry. Before he had boarded the bus, he had bought the *Times,* as always, but he was unable to concentrate on the news. His thoughts went back to Saturday evening, as they had throughout the week end. He let them—hanging to a strap, pushed against the other passengers; he let himself go over it all again.

He remembered that brief moment in the lobby of the Roosevelt when he and Billy were waiting for the girls to come from the ladies' room. Billy had made the remark: "It's a dreadful name—Charity—isn't it? But I adore her all the same!"

Adam had read in some psychology book that if the person became dear, the name became dear.

Billy had said: "Charity Cadwallader—it's like the name some novelist would give a rich girl, isn't it? Ah well, three-fourths of life is all clichés anyway."

"So she's rich, too," Adam had said.

"Very! She has the best kind of wealth, inherited."

"Just like you."

"Only more."

"Oh."

Billy had looked surprised; then he had laughed. "Good Lord, you actually sound disappointed. You weren't thinking of asking her for a—" but the girls had returned then.

The rain came harder and hit the panes of the bus in sharp needles. Adam wondered if she were sleeping still. Weren't all rich girls still asleep at quarter to eight in the morning? He thought of her long, black-as-night hair, spilled across a very white and soft pillow; and he remembered the simply-cut, elegant black suit she had worn Saturday night, and the infinitesimal gold watch on her wrist. She had worn tiny, pearl, pin-head earrings, and a smile which was polite, as though it disowned the penetrating green eyes that were watching Adam throughout their hour together.

Billy and Dorothy Schackleford had monopolized the conversation—Billy patronizing Dorothy almost as if to say to Adam that he was not impressed by Adam's story of success; that his way of showing it was to encourage Dorothy in more of her ordinary and naïve palaver. Adam had found no opportunity to explain why the part-owner of the Fifty-seventh Street Autograph Mart was dating a girl like Dorothy, and Billy was making the most of the fact Adam had such a girl with him.

For some small space of time, Billy had succeeded in making Adam uncomfortable with this maneuver. Dorothy had a very unfeminine way of discussing various physical ailments in frank detail, and Adam had squirmed while she told of a stomach disorder she suffered in Rome. At one point, in the midst of one of Dorothy's sentences, Adam had broken in, slapping the *Stammbuch* to the table in a clumsy and tactless gesture. With a slight nervous break to his voice, which made the tone nearly shrill, he had exclaimed: "Look here, Billy, I guess *you* can figure what this is worth! It's mine, a little present I bought for myself from our stock at The Mart."

Billy had enthused in his predicative, condescending way, as though he were patting Adam's head. Then he had resumed the conversation with Dorothy, and Dorothy picked it up with more elaboration on what it was like to have "the trots."

It was somewhere in the middle of it all, that Adam became aware of Charity's eyes watching him. It was then that he stopped caring about Dorothy or Billy. It became a small matter that Billy was goading Dorothy into more banality, with the express purpose of humiliating Adam. He was nearly sure that Charity was not even listening and had not been. What she was thinking—even what she thought of Adam—he had no way of divining, but he was hypnotized by a certain mood of calm.

Afterwards, Adam had said to Dorothy Schackleford: "She was staring at me. Did you notice?"

"She was an awful dummy," Dorothy had answered. "She had absolutely *nothing* to say!"

As they were leaving the table, while Billy walked ahead and the girls went to the ladies' room, Adam had pocketed a slip of paper Charity had wadded up and tossed in the ashtray. When Adam looked at it later, he saw that it was simply a receipt for a watch repair job from a shop on Madison Avenue. Save for one thing, it was unimportant, but the one thing was interesting to Adam. Her signature. The tops of her *a*'s were all closely knotted, an indication of extreme secretiveness, evidenced again in the fact that the upstroke of her *d* was separated from the downstroke. The signature was not much to go on, but Adam had little else. That Monday morning he did not even have reason to believe that he would ever encounter Charity Cadwallader again.

There was a light burning in The Mart when Adam arrived, and the stale and too-sweet smell of Mrs. Auerbach's rum. Before Adam did anything else, he put the *Stammbuch* back in the safe. Then he walked across to the card table, threw an empty rum bottle in the wastebasket, and looked through the clutter of papers piled there. Sometimes in her drunkenness Mrs. Auerbach had a moment of lucidity when she would wrote Adam a note instructing him to do this or that, which invariably should have been done long ago, or already was done. Usually the latter, for Adam knew the working of The Mart thoroughly. Just occasionally her reminders were important, and often, nearly illegible. But instead of instructions that Monday morning, Adam found a piece of old yellow paper, across which at the top Mrs. Auerbach had printed LAST WILL AND TESTAMENT.

She must have been even more drunk when she wrote it than she had been when Adam left her. The printed words ran into one another, and the letters were of varying sizes:

I leave my business to my assistant Adam Blessing who must run it and not sell it. That is a law! All my money to him too, and the Stammbuch of Johann Wolfgang von Goethe's son. If I die, it is the City of New York who kills me. If Adam Blessing dies, all goes to the Universal Committee on Conversation. That is a law and God's will, so be it. Ada Auerbach, her signature. May, 1958.

Mrs. Auerbach's *a*'s were all closely knotted at the top, too. Adam had noticed that about her handwriting before, and he had often thought of the fact she seldom discussed her past. But this morning it was simply another reminder of Charity Cadwallader.

For a moment while he held the yellow paper in his hand, Adam wished the old woman really was dead. But Adam knew full well *his* sort of luck. Mrs. Auerbach would live another twenty years, and write a different will each year, and Adam would probably be still making the same salary. He thought of his copy of the *Times* which he had not yet looked at, and he promised himself that when he did look at it, he would go through the Help Wanted advertisements. He felt suddenly angry at Mrs. Auerbach. The will, like her gift of the *Stamm-buch,* was another one of her meaningless gestures, forgotten even now as she snored through the morning rain, resting her huge fat self for another bout with the bottle, another of her harangues at five o'clock when Adam wanted to go home after a hard day's work. On an impulse which even Adam recognized as pointless, he folded the yellow paper and put it in his pocket.

Some rain had come in through the mail slot, so that when Adam picked up the morning's delivery, he found the ink smeared on several envelopes. On one, addressed to Adam, he noticed the *M*'s in "Mr." and "Mart," the high first stroke of the letter—mark of the arrogant social climber. He guessed that it was from that Mr. Clay on East Seventy-second Street, the customer who was so interested in owning a set of the autographs of Virginia's first families. When he looked at the return address on the envelope, his hands rushed to tear it open. It was from Billy.

Dear Addie:

You never told me where you lived, so I'm writing you at your business. When I returned to my apartment Saturday, I received a cable informing me that my father is very ill in Switzerland. I had been planning to go abroad for a year in September, but I must now leave immediately. Tuesday, in fact.

Some friends from Naples are taking my place in September, but it will be empty until then. I remember your mentioning that you were looking for a bigger apartment. Perhaps you could use mine until September, rent-free, of course. You would be doing me a favor, for I do not like to leave it empty, and you could forward my mail and pass on to phone-callers my situation. It is a large apartment with a garden. Would you call me the moment you get this, at EX 4-6161? It's a private listing, so don't lose this.

It was fun running into you last night.

Yours,
Billy.

A smile lingered on Adam's face after he folded the letter so that the phone number showed. He wondered what Billy would think if he knew that Adam's "place" was a barren-looking seventeen-dollar-a-week room in the Sixty-third Street YMCA. He could move into Billy's immediately, and he realized with a pleasant shock of surprise that Tuesday was tomorrow.

Adam tossed the rest of the mail on the card table, and walked, with a new spring to his step, toward the phone in the storeroom. He had the distinct feeling that he was on the threshold of a new way of life, that things were definitely taking a turn. He snapped on the light-button in the storeroom. It was then, at precisely 8:22 that rainy morning at the beginning of May, that he saw Mrs. Auerbach hanging from a piece of rope. The chair she had kicked away from her was overturned on the storeroom floor.

4

"Getting thin took all my will power. I managed it, but not while the Bollins were living in Auburn. After they moved away. I was eighteen the summer of my new self. I was 145 lbs! So proud! The only one—or at least the first one I wanted to see me, was Marshall Bollin. I knew Billy was off in Europe, so I traveled the 90 miles to Rochester. I pretended to be just passing through. I called on Marshall Bollin, still my idol—though I had not seen him in three years . . . He not only did not recognize me (that could have been my new appearance) but even after I said my name, he did not recall me right away. When he did, he had only vague recollections. 'Weren't you from the Home?' he said . . . I wonder if I'll ever forget how I felt at that moment? But I'm at it again, aren't I? Dwelling in the past! Damn!

FROM ADAM BLESSING'S JOURNAL

On Tuesday morning the sun came out at last. Adam basked in it out in Billy's garden. The Mart was closed due to Mrs. Auerbach's death. Adam had made arrangements for her cremation yesterday, and in last evening's newspaper there was a U.P. human interest piece on her death. Adam soaked up the hot sun and reread the article, sipping a Bloody Mary. The headline said: VICTIM OF A CHANGING CITY.

She was an eccentric. It was no secret that she kept thousands of dollars in cash in her apartment; no secret that she kept daily rendezvous with a rum bottle. In this city of lacerated minds, she could easily have been the victim of a robbery. She could just as well have become another pedestrian fatality in traffic statistics, as she made her way home unsteadily each evening down Fifty-seventh Street, crossing Park, Lexington and Third Avenues. Many ways were possible for Ada Auerbach, age 67, to become a victim of this huge, busy, often cruel metropolis. And so she was its victim.
"If I die, it is the City of New York who kills me." These were the words she had written in a suicide note. Police were summoned to The Autograph Mart yesterday morning by Adam Blessing, age 24, who found her in the shop's storeroom. He told police . . .

Adam did not finish rereading the clipping. It gushed on about lonely city dwellers and their private universes, taking several pokes at the way the City was tearing down residences to erect office buildings; and it teased the reader with descriptions of the sardine tins in Mrs. Auerbach's icebox, all of which contained a sum of $37,000; and of Mrs. Auerbach's strange ways, as recounted by neighbors and neighborhood tradesmen.
Adam folded it and put it in the pocket of his shirt. Yesterday, an hour or so before Adam had moved his bags from the YMCA to Billy's, a lawyer had told Adam Mrs. Auerbach's will would probably hold up. He had sat up with Billy until all hours last night, but the more he discussed his plans with Billy, the more it seemed like all the other times he talked with Billy, as though none of it was true. When Billy went, Adam supposed,

it would seem more real. At the moment, the only thing real was Adam's terrible hangover. It dulled the larger thoughts. The new world which Adam was about to realize seemed to be beginning as he had once read, in a poem, that the world would end—not with a bang, but a whimper.

Adam finished his Bloody Mary and set it on the flagstone beside the deck divan, where he was lying with his legs stretched out.

Always, Adam had thought he would love a garden, and it was somehow typical that Billy would hate it; typical that Adam had read books on gardening without any hope of having a garden of his own; typical that Billy had said last night: "You want to have drinks out *there*? Hell, Addie, there are bugs and soot, and it's a pain in the ass, Addie!"

It had been a concession to Adam that Billy had finally agreed to nightcaps in the garden; a "going-away gift," as Billy had put it; and it was also typical that it was Billy who was going away; Billy giving Adam the gift because Adam was not going away. . . . Trust Billy to live like *this* in New York City, Adam thought. Three-and-a-half rooms, the garden, and an address off Fifth in the Nineties—all for a piddling $140 a month. By Billy's standards, anyway, it was a piddling drop-in-the-bucket rent; by city standards the apartment was a find. And by Adam's standards? . . . A question mark. . . . "The way it looks now," the lawyer had told Adam, "it most probably will be a sizeable sum, but it's going to take time, you know. Probate court works slowly, and there are taxes to figure out, the usual red tape. . . . Don't make any big changes in your life just yet, that's my advice."

Adam smiled, leaned his head back and felt the sun's warmth. He could wait. . . . Last night when he was telling Billy about his plans, he had practiced great patience and restraint. After all, Billy did not know the true story. Billy thought Adam was already part-owner of The Mart, already something of a success. That was another reason none of it seemed real to Adam yet; he had had to maintain the pose.

Inside, Billy was telephoning.

". . .thought I'd buzz you before I took off," Adam could hear him say. "Idlewild at two-fifty, yes. . . . It's premature because of Father, but I expect I'll keep to the same itinerary after Switzerland. . . . No, I'm not going *near* Rome this year. Tired of it; you know how it is."

Adam dropped his cigarette on the flagstone, letting his leg swing down and rub it out. He had always dreamed of going to Europe. Now that it was going to be possible, Adam supposed he should dream of being tired of Rome one day. . . . That was Billy's style, all right. Tired of this, tired of that; his money made him tired, was all. Last night Adam had sampled one of Billy's French cigarettes. Billy was tired of the bland American kind, he had told Adam. The cigarette had nearly turned Adam's stomach with its harshness. Adam had remarked favorably on it, and smoked it down to the end. He felt that Billy was rather pleased with Adam's entire demeanor as they drank their nightcaps. Much more about Adam than his obvious loss of weight surprised Billy, Adam felt. Without any of Billy's advantages, Adam Blessing was a far cry from "Fatty Addie" of Auburn, New York. Wasn't that what Billy thought?

As Adam sat up to light a cigarette, he glanced at his watch again. It seemed that these hours before Billy's departure were interminable. As Adam smoked, he became aware of sudden noise. In the garden adjoining Billy's, he saw half a dozen young boys romping around, some on swings, some in sandpiles; one yanking at the fence separating the gardens. With them were a man and woman, standing by an iron slide, observing them.

"I forgot to tell you about *that!*" said Billy's voice behind Adam. Billy crossed the garden carrying a fresh pitcher of Bloody Marys. He poured Adam's glass full, and set the pitcher on the marble-top table. *"That,"* he said in an annoyed tone, "is King School. Oh, don't worry; it's a day school for one thing. And it closes for the summer the second week in June."

Billy was fastening his cuff links to his shirt, the same ones with the simple, soft-printed *B* embellishing their faces. They had come from Olga Tritt, Billy had told him last night; they were 22 karat, worth, Billy guessed, about $150. Charity Cadwallader had given them to Billy. He had told Adam that while they were having their nightcaps, Billy with his Sulka tie loosened and his collar unbuttoned, Adam with his tie knotted neatly and his coat on. Ostensibly, Adam could have been the apartment's occupant, and Billy the outsider, Adam was thinking that as he listened to Billy's bragging—as he watched Billy's appearance grow sloppier while they drank. Yet at a later point in the evening, Adam had realized his own speech was a trifle thick; he knew he was much higher than Billy was. When Billy suggested they "call it a night," he was polite enough to say "we've" had enough. It was the first thing Adam had remembered when he woke up in Billy's bedroom. As Adam recalled Billy's condescending way of ending their evening, he vowed that even if he had to sit home by himself and drink night after night, he would acquire a greater tolerance for liquor. *That* was something he had neglected. Billy Bollin had been holding cocktails and highballs in his hand since he was seventeen. He needed no practice.

Now as Adam regarded Billy standing there in the garden, he felt a certain sense of scorn, striped with a heady feeling of superiority. Acquiring a tolerance for liquor was perhaps just a worm's step in the direction Adam wanted to go. He would go past Billy, in that way and in every way. He envied Billy's herring-bone-pattern silk tweed suit, silver gray with the black slub and the long roll to the lapels, but he decided that he would never imitate Billy's taste in anything. Adam would be ultraconservative, just as Billy's father was. If Charity Cadwallader ever gave Adam a gift, Adam would not mention the shop it had come from, the karats, and certainly not the cost. That thought of Adam's was followed by a sudden, sharp headache.

"Is there any aspirin in your medicine cabinet, Billy?"

Billy said, "I have a prescription for something much better. Fix you up in no time, Addie. It's in a blue jar on the right."

That too, Adam mused as he crossed the garden, was somehow like Billy, to have a special headache pill, unavailable without a prescription.

In the living room, Adam stepped over Billy's luggage. All of it was plastered with customs' stamps and stickers from those hotels listed in guidebooks under "Luxury Class." Adam decided that when he *did* go to Europe, as soon as the money came through, he would stay in all the best places, and he would not allow anyone to put stickers on his baggage. He would swing to the opposite pole; be unostentatious about everything.

Last night with a bravado afforded by about seven-and-a-half drinks, Adam had asked Billy about Charity Cadwallader.

"Charity?" Billy had said in an off-hand way. "We're just friends now."

Adam had said that he thought she was quite pretty and that she had seemed very interesting. He did not know why he was unable to use the word "beautiful," instead of the bland understatement. The word interesting was not appropriate either, since she had hardly spoken to him, but he wanted to avoid saying something as dull as "nice."

Billy had jiggled his glass of bourbon thoughtfully for a moment, watching the ice cubes swish around. Then he had said, "I take it you're not serious with this Schackle-what's-her-name?"

"Not at all."

"Nor any girl in particular, ah?"

"I don't know any."

There was another brief pause, and then finally Billy said it right out. "Charity's family is very—well—prominent, Addie. . . . I guess one would have to know Charity about five years before even so much as walking her to the corner for a soda. In their view, anyway."

"She's free, white and twenty-one," Adam had said foolishly, sounding angry when he wanted most to sound simply matter-of-fact.

Billy had looked at him with a very wise tip to his lips: "Addie, you know that has nothing to do with it! You know full well what I'm telling you."

Adam immediately protested that he had meant nothing by his questions about Charity; the last thing in the world, he had declared staunchly, that he had on his nind was asking her out. But he knew he sounded completely unconvincing. It was shortly after that point in the evening when he began to show his drinks.

The phone rang while Adam was in the bathroom getting something for his headache, and once again Adam could hear Billy bubbling into the mouthpiece . . . about leaving Idlewild at two-fifty . . . about not going *near* Rome this time . . . then about Adam. Adam leaned against the door, which was ajar, and listened.

"Actually, I've known him all my life," Billy was saying, "We grew up back in Auburn. Haven't seen him in years, then we ran into each other a day or so ago. He's a nice enough fellow. He was an orphan. Used to cut our lawn . . . No, nothing like *that*. He has *some* polish. . . . Anyway, he's certainly reliable."

Certainly capable of watering the plants and forwarding the mail, Adam thought bitterly, even though he couldn't take Charity Cadwallader to the corner for a soda.

Adam swallowed two of the pills and walked back to the garden after Billy finished with the phone call. Billy was pouring yet another Bloody Mary, and Adam was already feeling his. Adam sat down beside Billy, wishing suddenly that he knew some friends he could ask by for drinks after Billy went. Crazily he realized that the one person he would have liked to ask by for a drink in an apartment like this, was Billy Bollin himself.

"Look over there," Billy was saying now. He pointed to the small boy whom Adam had noticed earlier, the one yanking at the fence separating the gardens. The youngster wore glasses which were incredibly thick, and he was shouting something. Billy held his finger to his lips in a shushing gesture.

"*Regardez* Timmy Schneider everybody!" the youngster was calling. "*Regardez* Timmy Schneider!"

Billy snickered. "He's always yelling that. The whole bunch of them are psychos."

Adam said, "What do you mean?"

Billy wiggled his finger in circles by his ear. "Nuts. *You* know. Crazy."

"Is it a hospital?"

"No, it's King School. It's a school for difficult children. They're all bats."

Adam looked across and through the fence at the children. They seemed to range in age from eight to thirteen. The iron slide, the swings, the sandpiles reminded him of the play yard at the Home.

"They look all right," he said.

Billy said, "Oh, they're not morons or anything like that. But they all have something crazy about them."

"It looks like the Home."

"Addie-boy, it's a far cry from the Cayuga County Orphans' Home. Those kids were born with silver spoons in their mouths, never mind the bats in the belfry. That one I pointed out—the one with the goggles, for instance. Does the name Schneider mean anything to you?"

"No." Adam felt suddenly tired. Perhaps it was thinking of the Home again, being able to visualize it so well after seeing the back yard of King School.

"Well, Luther Van den Perre Schneider is the kid's old man. That little fellow with the goggles, Addie-boy, is heir to millions. Sole heir, I might add. And he's cracked."

Adam had a dizzy sensation all through him. He hoped Billy would not notice anything was wrong. He managed to say, "How do you know all this?"

"My maid gets it from their cook. This will hand you a laugh," said Billy, tapping Adam's wrist. "My maid told me they punish those kids by making them sit out in the hall until they can be good. My maid says the halls are filled with kids sitting there masturbating." Billy hooted over his own story. "My maid didn't put it that way exactly. She said the kids sat in the hall 'touching their privates.' "

Adam felt unbelievably dopey. He tried to laugh at Billy's joke, but he could barely grin. He felt his eyes want to close, and he forced them to remain open.

"Luther Schneider owns Waverly Foods," Billy said.

Those were the last words Billy Bollin spoke to Adam Blessing for over a year.

5

"Marshall Bollin chose me as the orphan he would be nice to, in a random way, I suppose. He probably took my name from the top of the list, since the names were arranged alphabetically and I was the very first. Actually I saw very little of him. On those days I was asked to the Bollins', Billy entertained me. I cannot help thinking my whole life would have been different if Marshall Bollin had not had a son. Then he might even have adopted me. I used to dream that something awful had happened to Billy, and that Mr. Bollin came to the Home and asked me to be his son.

FROM ADAM BLESSING'S JOURNAL

Adam was dreaming. Mrs. Auerbach was hanging by the rope in the storeroom. He took a knife from his pocket to cut her down. When he looked up at her, she was scaling a fence. He followed her. Then he hung to the fence. Below him was Billy Bollin.

"*Regardez* Adam Blessing!" Adam shouted.

Billy made circles around his ear with his finger. "You're cracked, Addie," he said. . . . Adam thought: This is only a dream, and promptly woke up.

He was stretched out on the deck divan in Billy's garden. He was shoeless, and his tie was loosened. It was not yet full evening, but the sun was down, and the chill of a dusk in early May made him shiver. His headache was even worse than his instant anxiety at what had happened. As he got up and crossed the flagstone, he had to hold his head with both hands to ease the pain.

He found the light switch in the living room. There in the room's center was a piece of white typing paper on the rug, a large bottle of Remy Martin holding it down. As carefully as he could manage, jarring his head as little as possible, Adam bent over and picked it up.

Addie, you took the wrong pills, buddy! You took the ones in the white bottle. They're for sleeping.

Pleasant dreams.

Please pass on the enclosed itineraries to friends who call. It'll be effective as of June third, if father is all right. I hope you straighten out everything at The Mart. If you need any special legal assistance, my lawyer's name is on my phone pad. I wouldn't trust any lawyer recommended by the YMCA, but that's your business.
So long, B. B.

Attached with staples were several mimeographed sheets with the heading: TENTATIVE ITINERARY OF WILLIAM COVINGTON BOLLIN THROUGH SEPTEMBER.

Adam sank into the soft folds of the living-room couch, dropping Billy's note and the itineraries on the pillow beside him. He was still quite groggy. His mind seemed unable to focus on anything but thoughts that strayed into senseless daydreams. He imagined his lawyer phoning to tell him the will was invalid; then imagined himself calling Billy's lawyer; imagined Billy's lawyer saying snidely: "But I thought you were part-owner of the business! You mean you were just a clerk?" . . . Then his thoughts concentrated on a plan whereby Billy's itineraries would become misplaced, so that none of his friends would be able to communicate with him. He imagined Billy's face, as day by day there was no mail for him. Billy was always so keen on the number of friends he had. . . . He started a new daydream about Billy's sleeping pills having killed Adam, and Billy being tried for his murder. The prosecuting attorney was saying to Billy: *Isn't it a fact, Mr. Bollin, that you were always bullying the deceased when you were growing up with him back in Auburn, New York?* Before Billy could offer his defense, the phone rang. He leaped up.

"Hello!" said a girl's voice. "I'm calling Adam Blessing. Is he there?"

"I'm Adam Blessing." For one self-deluded half-second, a fierce hope sprang up in Adam, but it was only Dorothy Schackleford calling.

Adam sank onto a white-and-gold Empire chair, sighing.

"Well, *you* sound enthusiastic. You'd think I was the local funeral director."

"Very funny," said Adam.

"Oh, gosh, Adam—I'm sorry. I keep forgetting Mrs. Auerbach."

Adam said, "Oh well, it doesn't matter. . . . It's over now."

"I got your number from the Y, Adam. Did you move already? Didn't you go to work today?"

Adam told her about Billy's offer, and as he did, he listened to her squeals of delight with a certain uneasiness. There was just enough about Dorothy Schackleford which was like Adam, to make him annoyed by her.

"Off Fifth!" she was exclaiming. "Ver-ree-rit-zee!" whistling for emphasis.

Her rhapsodic reaction made Adam tighten. "It's not so grand," he said, "and furthermore I can afford the same now." He stared across the room at a forgotten dirty breakfast plate which Billy had left under a velvet-covered chair. An Etrusan chair, Billy had called it, or what was it? Etriscan? Etruscan? . . . Tomorrow he would go to the library and take out a book on furniture.

". . . so I'm going to move in with these girls," Dorothy Schackleford was chattering on. "You can't live with your family all your life, can you, Adam?"

Adam said he guessed not.

"Nothing gets a rise out of you, Adam . . . I'm sorry. I know you still must feel just awful about Mrs. Auerbach!"

Adam felt like telling her that he did not feel anything about Mrs. Auerbach. He had tried, but it was hopeless.

"I have the perfect housewarming gift for you, Adam," Dorothy was continuing. "A Pan-Trans ticket agent got me two forks and two spoons from the Excelsior in Rome. I'll give you a pair."

"Thank you," Adam said.

"You really are taking it badly, aren't you, Adam?"

"No, I'm not," said Adam. "I'm just—tired."

"Your voice is funny."

"Tired." Adam repeated.

"I was wondering Adam . . . I know tomorrow's a weekday and all, but, at this place I'm moving into, we're having a little impromptu get-together tonight. Have you eaten?" Before he could answer, she forged ahead. "Oh, it's nothing much—just spaghetti and a tossed salad, and we'll be sitting around drinking wine and all, but I thought maybe you'd—" and her voice trailed off.

"I don't think so, thanks."

"I suppose the people wouldn't interest *you*. I mean, *any more.*"

"Don't be silly. It isn't that."

"We haven't even got all our furniture either."

"That wouldn't bother me, Dorothy."

"Adam . . . I agree with you about imitation fire-places now."

"What?"

"That time you criticized my girlfriend for having an imitation fireplace, remember? Well, I know I was awfully mad, but you were right, Adam."

Adam said, "What do I know about furniture? I was just drunk that night."

"These girls I'm moving in with aren't like that, Adam, honest! They've all been abroad. I mean, they all work for the airlines. I guess they're not big intellectuals or anything but—"

"Sometime I'd like to meet them," Adam lied.

"I just thought tonight would be nice."

"Dorothy," said Adam, and in the next breath Adam told her he would be there, shortly after seven.

After he hung up, he realized that the few times he had been out with Dorothy, *she* had asked *him*. He had always begun with a refusal and ended up accepting. Each time, too, he had vowed it would be the last time, but against a girl of Dorothy Schackleford's ilk Adam had no more chance of keeping that vow than the Excelsior had of keeping its silverware.

Until his headache subsided, Adam read for a while. It was a guide to Rome he had found in Billy's bookcase. He read an elaborate description of the gardens in the Pincio there, and he began to feel better. He thought that tomorrow he would perhaps arrange for a small memorial service for Mrs. Auerbach. He supposed very few people would even attend, but some of the merchants on Fifty-seventh might send representatives as a token gesture, and he might look up a few of her neighbors that would come, if only out of curiosity. Mrs. Auerbach would probably have hated such an idea, but Adam felt he ought to do something.

As he dressed for the evening, Adam was unable to resist wearing a pair of Billy's cuff links. They were in the shape of poodles, with ruby eyes, and Adam was amused and pleased by them. He also chose one of Billy's Countess Mara ties to wear, and these additions to his wardrobe gave him a lift. On an impulse, he also pocketed a package of Gauloises, Billy's French cigarettes.

At Ninety-sixth and Madison, Adam paused at a newsstand to buy a copy of *Art News*. The inspiration for this choice he could trace back to his conversation with Billy last night in the garden. Billy had said he hoped to visit The Prado in Madrid.

"You know," Billy had said, "they have the best Bosch in the world."

Adam had thought he meant the soup, borscht; he had thought the Prado was a restaurant. He had made some stupid comment about thinking Russia was more famous for it, adding that he had tasted it several times in the Russian Tea Room, right here in New York. Billy had choked with guffaws, apologizing as he choked, and ended by explaining in a very supercilious way that Hieronymus Bosch was a fifteenth-century painter; that The Prado was one of the most famous museums in the world.

"It's not your fault, Addie," Billy had said, still trying to stop laughing. "I wouldn't expect you to know about things like that."

Adam had smarted under the ridicule. Before he had fallen into bed last night, he had drunkenly scribbled,

"Learn more about ART," across a back page of his
Journal. Above it, in a sober script, there was a sentence which he had copied from *Of Human Bondage,*
after he had read it two years ago: "Money is like a
sixth sense, without which you cannot make use of the
other five. . . ."

On the bus, and then on the subway, Adam tried to
concentrate on the magazine. Instead he found himself
wondering about Charity Cadwallader. With the fatuous
license of the daydreamer, he found himself honey-
mooning with her in Rome. He saw himself walking into
the Pincio with her, seeing it all as it had been described
in the travel guide. He sat across from her in the Casino
Valadier, while they sipped sherry, with the swallows
darting about the balcony terrace, and the superb view
of Rome in the distance. He heard himself suggesting a
walk along the edge of the Piazzale del Pincio, and he
felt her hand tighten in his as they stood looking up at
a summer sky, as pink as flamingo feathers.
The subway jerked to a shaky stop at One Hundred
Eighty-first Street, just as Adam was kissing Charity by
the Fountain of Moses.
As he made his way through the dank underground
station, he decided a honeymoon in Rome would probably only bore a Charity Cadwallader.
"Everyone's going to Russia these days," Billy had
said last night, "or the Orient! . . . Europe's been had!
I suppose this will be my last trip there."
He tried to imagine himself somewhere in the Orient
on his honeymoon with Charity, but even in dreams he
was a captive of his limited experience. The Orient
looked oddly like the pictures Adam had seen of Europe, and when he tried to fill in for himself, everything
looked like upstate New York. He could see Charity
Cadwallader yawning in his mind's eye, as he went
through the subway stile.
When he arrived at Dorothy Schackleford's, Dorothy
was already a little high. Her lipstick was worn away
and there was a purple wine mark along her lower lip.
She was wearing toreador pants and a Venetian gondo-

lier's shirt; she was barefoot and her toenails were painted scarlet.

"Adam!" she said, gripping his hand in a hearty shake, "*Alors,* Adam! *Entrez! Mucho* welcome, *Adamo!*"

There were sling chairs and burlap curtains, and Chianti bottles with candles stuck in them; bare floors, and few people. Everyone was playing Charades; everyone was assigned to a team. Dorothy handed him a paper cup of sweet port, and Adam sat on a pillow on the floor, until the round of Charades was over.

On the glass-top coffee table beside him, there was the ashtray from the Stork Club, which Adam had given Dorothy. There was one from Maxim's in Paris, too, and the matchbooks on display were from places in Germany, Switzerland, Italy and France. . . . For some reason, a girl opposite Adam was answering *"Mais oui!"* to everything; and beside her, another girl was wearing a Japanese kimono. Adam and a chubby, bespectacled young man with a bald head, were the only males present.

After Charades, someone put on "Gypsy." The fat man danced with the girl who said *"Mais oui,"* and Dorothy turned to Adam and smiled. *"Alors,"* she said, *"wie gehts?"*

"Fine," said Adam.

Dorothy pointed to the girl in the Japanese kimono. "Remember her, Adam?"

"No."

"That's Shirley Spriggs. We ran into her one night at the Blue Mill. Remember that night we went to the Village for steaks?"

"I guess so," said Adam.

"Poor Shirl," Dorothy said, without elaborating. *"Beaucoup* troubles."

Adam could think of no response. He noticed as Dorothy sat with her bare legs crossed, that the soles of her feet were black with dust. Wine was spilled down the Venetian gondolier's shirt, and the nailpolish on her right hand was chipped. He remembered suddenly that Charity Cadwallader had worn no nailpolish; that her hands were long and soft-looking, clean and quiet.

"Hey, did you meet Norman yet?" Dorothy pointed at

the other male present. He and his partner were busy with the Charleston.

"Norman's in tickets at World-Wide," said Dorothy. "I met him in Madrid two summers ago when I got my three weeks off. Course only one week was with pay, but I took the other two. He really has a fabulous sense of humor. *Très* funny, is Norman."

Adam said, "He's good for a fat boy."

"I don't think that's very nice, Adam."

"I didn't mean anything by it."

"Norman's sensitive about his weight. He's tried everything."

"Look, I was fat once. I was very clumsy. I just meant—"

"*His* is glandular," Dorothy Schackleford persisted. "He couldn't do anything about it if he wanted to."

"I'm sorry."

"Sometimes you're really not very nice, Adam. You think you're better than most people just because you read up on things."

"That's not true," Adam began, but before he was able to finish, Shirley Spriggs came across in her kimono, and threw her arms around Adam as though they had always known one another as fast friends.

"You be nice to Shirl while I fix my face," Dorothy told Adam.

After she left, Adam asked Shirley Spriggs to dance. Immediately, he regretted it. The invitation was declined, but it had succeeded in launching her on a long explanation of why she was not going to dance for two years. It was a tribute to someone who was dead.

"It was Flight 791 out of Shannon," she said, "and it could just as well have been me, Adam. I knew Ginger Klein like I knew my own mother, only of course she was *my* age, and she was engaged and everything to this dentist. She had a half-a-karat diamond he gave her right on her wedding finger when the plane went down, and a wallet she bought him in Florence and everything —all lost in the ocean, and it was going to be her seventy-sixth trip too, and after that she was going to marry; well, when I think of it—" and she was unable to continue for a few moments. Adam lent her his handkerchief, and he realized she was rather high as well; quite drunk, in fact. Her next words were thick and teary: "It was one of those fweak—freak things, plane just blew up; we face it every trip but never think—" she could not finish.

Dorothy Schackleford flew across the room to guide Shirley Spriggs into the bathroom.

"Gingy wouldn't want you to break down like this, Shirl," she said. "You know how Gingy was."

Adam lighted a Gauloise and some seconds later the boy named Norman wandered over with the girl who said *"Mais oui."* Her name was Rose Marie Scoppettone, which meant "big gun" in Italian, she said; and then she said: "What smells like manure?"

"My cigarette," said Adam. "It's a Gauloise." As he looked about him at the collection of foreign matchbooks and ashtrays, he wished suddenly that he had bought his own pack of Chesterfields. Birds of a feather, he thought tiredly.

Norman said, "Oh, I thought it might be a dung-hill," at which all the girls giggled, inspiring him to repeat the quip three more times.

Adam danced with a girl named Eloise Siden, who booked New York-Caracas, and smelled of garlic. She danced Adam off into a corner.

"Shirley's a mess," she said in a confidential tone, "Gingy Klein was her best friend. They were like sisters. Gingy was going to live with us. We got Dotty instead."

"Good," said Adam. "I mean, I'm glad you could get someone."

"You know, Dotty's got a case on you, mister."

"Me? She hardly knows me, Shirley."

"I'm Eloise, remember?"

"I'm sorry."

"I don't mind telling you she could be very serious about you, Adam."

"You must be mistaken, really."

"Listen, mister, *I* know! Dotty's a great girl too. A guy would be fortunate."

They were very nearly standing still as they moved to the music. Adam edged into a corner of the room.

Eloise Siden said, "You don't have a special girl or anything do you?"

"No," said Adam. "But—"

"Don't But with me, mister," she said out of the corner of her mouth, "I'm giving you the straight poop and I expect the same from you. I'm from Texas, and we don't fool around much down there."

"Well," said Adam, "I just don't know Dorothy well. I don't know her well at all."

"You don't think you're too good for her or anything like that, do you?"

Adam felt his face get red. "No," he said.

"I thought you might have that idea. I thought to myself, 'Kid, if that's what that fellow has up his nose, just toddle on over there and give him the word.' Okay," she said, squeezing his shoulder, "no hard feelings. I just want it down in the record, Adam."

Norman danced up beside them and said, "What brand cigarettes you smokin' pard'ner," grinning widely at Eloise Siden as he said it—"dung-hills?"

There was another round of guffaws; then the music was over and the girl whose name meant "big gun" in Italian was shuffling through the records for another L.P.

"I just hope Shirl's O.K.," said Eloise. "Boy, I mean, she was thrown for a looper by that plane crash."

"Why don't you go see?" said Adam.

"You know, that's a thought. A gooder!"

"Yes, go see."

"I'll be back *di*-rectly. Don't go away, friend!" She gave his shoulder another healthy squeeze, and winked meaningfully. "You and Dot's got to get to know one another better, right quick!"

The moment she turned, Adam made his way rapidly down the hall and out the door. He ran down the two flights of stairs, out into the street. Then he ran all the way to the One Hundred Eighty-first subway station.

Standing inside on the platform, while he waited for the D train, he mopped the perspiration off his face. He had left behind his copy of *Art News*. Momentarily, he studied the graffiti on the posters. He came to one which was the blow-up of that week's *Our Time* magazine—the picture of a man. Someone had drawn spectacles and a mustache on his face; someone else had scribbled across the face in red crayon: *His stuff stinks! Don't eat it! . . .* As the D train approached, Adam glanced down at the printing under the man's picture. It said:

LUTHER VAN DEN PERRE SCHNEIDER
WAVERLY FOODS: AN EMPIRE

At one Hundred Twenty-fifth Street, where Adam changed to a local, he bought a copy of *Our Time* from the vendor.

6

". . . and yet despite his robust appearance and his indefatigable approach to the management of Waverly Foods at all levels, 'Lute' Schneider is a somewhat solitary figure in his personal life. On one of the rare occasions when he granted permission for an interview, the reporter came away knowing far more about Schneider's silver collection than about his family, friends, or the complicated manipulations of his empire. Above all else, he seemed most enthusiastic about two possessions: a very rare, old English silver and tigerwear jug, and a Sheffield plate epergne on a revolving base; circa 1770.

Married seventeen years to society beauty Win Griswold, they have a son Timothy, age 9. Their town house in the East Nineties is . . ."

The sharp sound of the outside buzzer interrupted Adam's reading. His watch said eleven-thirty. The phone had rung four or five times since he had come back to the apartment that evening, but he had not bothered to answer it. He was convinced it was Dorothy Schackleford, calling to see why he had run off.

On the table beside Adam was a bottle of Clos de Vougeot, which he had taken from Billy's wine closet. Adam had already drunk a little more than half. As the ringing of the buzzer became more insistent, Adam crossed the living room determined to get rid of Dorothy Schackleford as quickly as he could. Pressing the release button, Adam was angry. He had been enjoying himself for the first time since Mrs. Auerbach's death. Sipping the wine and reading about Luther Schneider, the cool breeze from the garden wafting in on him, he had forgotten for a while about everything. A Gauloise hung from his lips. It was strange, he had a taste for them now.

He heard the noise of high heels on the black-and-white marble outside; then two bleeping rings of his doorbell. Before he opened the door, he loosened Billy's Countess Mara tie, and mussed up his hair, hoping the dishevelment would add credence to his story, that he was suddenly taken ill. A migraine, he would say, remembering how suddenly Mrs. Auerbach's migraines used to occur. So sure that it would be Dorothy Schackleford, Adam did not recognize his caller immediately.

"It's *you*," she said. "I thought it would be you."

Charity Cadwallader was not exactly smiling, but regarding him instead with a sort of amused curiosity. She was taller than Adam had remembered, or her heels were higher this time. Adam could not be sure whether she was slightly taller than he was. He was so stunned by her appearance there that his mind could fasten only on the insignificant particulars: she was wearing a different watch this time, a larger one, silver and shell-shaped; her black hair was pulled back in a chignon; and now he noticed the color of her eyes, green—like a cat's. Adam's fingers rushed to straighten his tie, smooth back his hair.

She was already inside the apartment. "I rang," she said, "two times. Don't you answer phones?"

"I thought it was someone else."

"I'm sorry, Addie, but Billy *promised* he'd drop off

my tennis racket before he left. I have a tennis date tomorrow.”

“I haven’t seen it here.” He hated her calling him “Addie” as Billy always did.

“It’s here, all right.” She glanced in the living room. “Billy got off all right?”

“Yes.”

“Earlier I saw the lights from the street. I didn’t know for sure who was staying here. Billy mentioned someone would be living here.”

“Would you like a drink?”

“I don’t like liquor, but Billy keeps celery tonic around. On the rocks, please.”

While he was breaking ice, she walked back and forth. “I hope Billy’s father’s all right. He’s very close to him, isn’t he?”

“I guess so.”

“Guess? . . . Billy always talks about him. Does he look like Billy?”

“Mr. Bollin was always ill. He’s sort of frail. He’s a little man.”

“Funny, I pictured him as a big, heavy sort.”

“He’s very kind, too.”

“And Billy isn’t.”

“I didn’t say that.”

Adam handed her a glass of celery tonic. “Do you live in the neighborhood, Charity?”

“Off Park, next block. . . . Billy told me about your partner’s death. I’m sorry.”

“Yes,” Adam said. “It was sudden. I’ll have a lot more responsibility now.”

Charity Cadwallader did not really sit down, but perched on the edge of the conch-shaped couch, as though she were having the drink on the run, with little enthusiasm.

She said, “Billy and you grew up together, hmmm?”

“I was an orphan. Some of the ‘better-off’ families in Auburn picked out an orphan to invite to dinner now and then. Mr. Bollin picked me.”

“What was Billy like?”

“Mean,” said Adam.

She laughed at that. “I’ll bet!”

"Did he ever tell you that he used to keep snakes? He had a regular herpetorium in his cellar. It was a reptile house as fancy as any zoo's."

"He said he used to like snakes. Tell me about it."

"He had this cobra," said Adam. "He called him 'Poopsy.' Poopsy ate six-foot black racers. Billy'd put one in the cage with Poopsy, and Poopsy's head would peer around a corner of the water tank, and then there'd be a motion like lightning. The black snake would make one desperate attempt for his life. He'd try to coil around Poopsy's throat, but before you knew it—you couldn't even see it, it was so fast—this black head would be caught in Poopsy's jaws, and Poopsy'd draw this fighting black snake inside him."

Charity Cadwallader had no particular expression on her face, merely listened.

"Poopsy'd pause for breath now and then in the process of eating him," Adam said, "but he'd get him down, inch by inch. . . . I used to stand there shaking, wet clear through my clothes from perspiration."

"I've never much liked snakes either," she said, "What else?"

"Billy used to tease me a lot. One day he was behaving very differently toward me. He was going to move soon, and he said since we wouldn't be seeing each other much, we ought to try to get along better. . . . Another thing about Poopsy, he wouldn't eat little snakes, only big ones. There were never enough big ones available, so Billy had to produce one artificially. He had a black-snake cage. Up in the top of this cage-tree, there'd be a whole bunch of little ones hanging. They were all twisted together like rain worms, all knotted up. Billy'd look for the biggest in the bunch, and then he'd disentangle them until he got it. I only saw him get bitten twice doing that. He was good at it."

Charity said, "I can imagine."

"He'd pull this snake out of the bunch, Charity, and then he'd hold him, squirming and wiggling by the tail." Adam looked into her eyes, wondering why she seemed completely bland about his story, not like most women when snakes were discussed. He said, "Then like the lash of a whip, Billy would whirl the thing through the air and there'd be a snap!"

"The snake would have a broken neck, is that it?"

"That's right."

"Then?"

"Then, Adam said, "Billy would stuff frogs down the dead snakes throat, to make him look bigger, so Poopsy would eat him.

"Very clever."

"Yes . . . clever." Adam wondered why he wished she had been afraid at the story, and not so cool and unconcerned.

"You were telling me about one day in particular."

"Not very interesting. You have to be afraid of snakes to know how I felt."

"Tell me."

"Billy said we were going to turn over a new leaf. He said he wanted me to help him feed Poopsy. More moral support than anything else. Usually the Bollin's chauffeur went along with Billy for the feeding, but it was the chauffeur's day off. I agreed to go along. Billy told me to turn my back, if I wanted to while he broke the black snake's neck."

"And you wanted to."

"Sure! Well, I told you! I was afraid of snakes."

"Go on."

"After I turned around, the next thing I knew, that snake was around my neck, and down my shirt, and I began to run up the stairs, trying to pull my shirt off, but mostly going crazy! I was really afraid of snakes."

"Yes," she agreed.

"You can't imagine what that's like unless you're afraid of them too."

"And then?"

"It turned out it was only a garter snake. It didn't bite me or anything. . . . But I didn't get over it for days. I remember I stayed for dinner at the Bollins' that night, but I couldn't eat. Billy's father knew something was wrong. He knew Billy pretty well. I wouldn't tell him what happened, but he knew, and I remember that before we went into the dining room that night, Mr.

Bollin put his arm around my shoulder and said: 'Adam,
I'd be very proud if you were my boy.' "

Charity did not say anything for a few seconds; then
she said, "And you always wished you were."

"No . . . I envied certain advantages Billy had."

"Money."

"Yes. Money."

"People with money fascinate you, don't they, Addie?"

"No. They don't *fascinate* me."

"But you like to read about people like Luther
Schneider?"

Adam blushed, picked up the copy of *Our Time* from
his chair, and put it beside the wine bottle on the table.
"I could have been reading any article in there."

"But your face is so red." There was a pause. She
did not smile. Then she changed the subject abruptly.
"I can't imagine you fat."

"I was . . . very. I ate cake all the time. I ate it when
I was terribly happy, and when I was very sad, and in
between because I felt neither way. I had to work like
the devil to get down to a normal weight. But I did it."

"Congratulations."

"Sarcasm?"

"No. I like people who are determined. . . . Now that
you've come into a little money, I suppose you'll cata-
pult it to millions, is that what you want to do with
your new inheritance?"

"Sure," said Adam, "I'm on my way to becoming
another Luther Schneider, or a Billy Bollin. How about
that?"

"Billy's in his twenties and has an ulcer, and Luther
Schneider has a son who's deranged and a wife who
drinks. What will you come down with?"

You, Adam wanted to say.

He said: "Money will do things *for* me, not *to* me. . . .
Besides, money didn't make Luther Schneider's boy
crazy, and I doubt that it made his wife drink. He enjoys his money, what's more. He collects fine silver,
raises orchids—before the war he even trained horses
that ran at Ouilly, in France. That doesn't sound like
a miserable existence!"

"It sounds as though you read the article in *Our Time* very, very thoroughly."

"You have me," Adam said.

Charity Cadwallader laughed for the first time. "Promises. Promises."

She had three more celery tonics before she called her home and left the message. The gist of it was that if her parents wanted to know where she was, she was staying with a girlfriend. Then she called the girlfriend, waking her up, making her promise to cover for her if anything should happen. Adam could hear both conversations from the garden.

When she rejoined him, she took the brandy snifter from his hand. "Don't drink any more, Addie. Wine and brandy don't mix."

"*Adam.*"

"All right—Adam."

She pulled him to his feet, and he felt her arms reach up around his neck, the same gentle way she had kissed him when she had first crossed the living room, a few hours earlier. He kissed her, slowly, thinking of nothing else, and she seemed to enjoy it with a certain calm. When he had first kissed her that night, he had blurted out a long speech about feeling a great warmth for her the first time he ever saw her, but she seemed uninterested in any declarations or clarifications, so he dropped it. They had talked about Billy, and she had said once quite emphatically that she hated Billy, but she would not elaborate.

After the kiss in the garden, she said, "You don't really want to finish your brandy, do you? It'll make you drunk, Adam."

They went inside, and it embarrassed Adam a little that she wanted him to take a shower with her first. In the shower, Adam realized that he was quite drunk already.

When he woke up in the morning he thought she was gone. Instead, she was in the kitchen making coffee, washing last night's glasses. He hurried into his pajamas and went out there, and she greeted him with a half smile. "Don't kiss me," she said when he came close to her. "I haven't brushed my teeth yet."

"I don't care."

"I do."

He leaned against the wall and watched her for a bit. Then he said. "Look, I'm sorry. I was just too drunk."

"It doesn't make any difference."

"These last few days have been upsetting, too."

"It happens all the time. Don't think about it."

"It doesn't happen to me," Adam lied.

"Well, it did last night," she said pleasantly. "Let's forget it. There's orange juice in the pitcher there. If there'd been fresh oranges I would have squeezed some. I'm afraid it's frozen."

"Are there any eggs?"

"None. Sorry."

"I'll slip on something and get some. Look, Charity, wouldn't you like a big breakfast?"

"All right."

"I won't be long," he said.

She said, "I'll have my shower while you're gone."

As Adam was leaving, the shower was running. He would buy sausages and rolls, he decided, and he would find some place where he could buy flowers. He took all the money he had with him, which was fifty-two dollars, the last of his cash. He knew why he took so much when he passed the jewelry store on Madison Avenue, after he left the grocery and the florist. He paid thirty-two dollars for a pearl teardrop on a tiny gold chain.

When he returned, she was gone. The note was on the kitchen table.

Dear Adam,
I just remembered my tennis date—at one o'clock. It's past noon now. I make eggs pretty well, and I would have liked making some for you. *C'est la vie.* Charity.

That was it.

He felt like weeping or punching something. Instead he left all his purchases, including the small bunch of violets and the jeweler's box, on the Etruscan chair in the living room, and he flopped on the unmade bed. He lighted a Gauloise, smoked it halfway down, then still in his clothes, hugged the pillow that smelled faintly of her perfume, and fell into a deep sleep. He dreamed of her in a fit of fifty or more snapshot glimpses, like the dream of someone drugged. When he woke up, he was perspiring in his clothes, the phone was ringing; it was after three in the afternoon.

"Hello, Adam?" said Dorothy Schackleford. "Are you all right?"

He was out of breath from his dash for the phone.

"I'm sorry I had to leave last night," he managed. "I had a migraine."

"We wondered what happened. Norman went looking for you and everything."

The robe of Billy's which Charity had been wearing was on the couch. He walked across and picked it up, carrying the telephone in his hand. He sat down and put the robe near his face, to smell it. Then, thinking of Billy's having worn it, he flung it to the floor.

"I'm sorry," he said.

"I thought you might be mad at *me*."

"It was a headache," he said. He suddenly remembered that Charity Cadwallader had cried last night; it was so vague he could not be positive, but he remembered himself saying not to cry. It was all blacked out then.

"I wouldn't have left you, Adam, but Shirl was real upset. You see, she and Gingy Klein were—"

"I know all that!"

"Don't bite my head off, Adam. I'm just trying to explain!"

"Never mind."

"You didn't go to work today either, did you?"

"No!" Adam said angrily.

"You're not very pleasant, Adam."

"I'm in a rush," said Adam, "I'm on my way out." He thought: the tennis racket: he had not even seen this tennis racket Charity had come for. He wondered if there was one, or if she had made it up.

"I thought you felt ill!"

"I'm going to the doctor!"

"Well, thanks a lot Adam, for being so nice. I have to get back to work now, but thanks a lot. I couldn't have spent my coffee-break in a nicer way."

"I'm sorry," he said.

"I'll never call you again, Adam."

Adam heard the click, then the dial tone.

While he was having some of the coffee Charity had made that morning, he remembered she had mentioned a luncheon she was going to at the Colony tomorrow. He took the coffee out into the garden, along with the Manhattan telephone directory. He smoked another Gauloise and balanced the directory on his lap. . . . Just as he had thought, there were no listings for any Cadwalladers in the Nineties, nor on Park Avenue, nor on Madison Avenue. He sat trying to think what she could have meant when she told him that she lived just around the corner . . . or had she said 'in the next block'? He smoked the last of the Gauloises and finished the coffee. In the adjacent yard the children were being let out to play, and momentarily he looked for the small boy with the thick glasses, the son of Luther Schneider. He could not seem to pick him out from the others. While he was watching the yard of the King School, his phone rang a second time. Adam Blessing nearly turned his ankle racing for it. It was the Bennan-Olicker Cremation Company. They wanted instructions for Mrs. Auerbach's remains.

7

GOOD THINGS TO KNOW:

1. *Rare, fancy restaurant: Ficklin's, East 59th Street. No sign out front. Dinners about $8 apiece. No liquor, but wine. No menu so don't make a fool of yourself by asking for one. Intimate, candlelit. Must have reservations.*

(Source: "A Sophisticated Guide to New York.")

2. *"The only red wines that may profitably be chilled are Beaujolais and Swiss Dôle."—from* Gourmet Cookbook.

FROM ADAM BLESSING'S JOURNAL

At noon on Thursday, Adam sold "The Lucy Baker Album" for $1500. He deposited $500 in his checking account, and $500 in the cash register of The Mart. $300 he put in his wallet. With the remainder he arranged for a small memorial service for Mrs. Auerbach, at a Unitarian church. The service was to be held that Saturday evening, and Adam spent the rest of Thursday notifying the merchants on Fifty-seventh, and tracking down a few former tenants from Mrs. Auerbach's building. He also bought himself a chalk-striped black wool worsted suit for the occasion. Mr. Geismar, Adam's lawyer, advised Adam to go more slowly, since Adam was still not Mrs. Auerbach's legal heir, but Adam felt Geismar was something of an old maid in his cautious attitudes.

At Wadley & Smythe, Adam paid for twenty dollars' worth of long-stem red roses. He remembered that Charity had said she was going to a luncheon at the Colony that noon. The flowers were to be delivered to her table. Adam enclosed the tiny pearl teardrop on the gold chain, and after considerable deliberation about what to write on the accompanying card, chose simply to say: "Always, Adam."

Before he closed The Mart that evening, he took care of several other things. He placed an advertisement in the *Times* for a helper, and he petitioned for membership in The Diners' Club. He ordered new stationery, with his own name printed on it, and the single word "owner" under his name. He made a draft of a letter to be sent to dealers, advising them of the availability of several albums Mrs. Auerbach had been loath to sell, and he cleared the premises of old rum bottles, and sundry trash can "souvenirs" Mrs. Auerbach had collected over the years.

It was after seven when Adam arrived at his apartment. Before he fixed himself a highball, he called the Colony to check whether the flowers had been presented to Charity. He was assured they had been, and as he sat out in the garden sipping some of Billy's Scotch, his sense of well-being was at its peak. Yesterday had been sloppy, all right—he had gotten off to a bad start —but that was over. Things were going along rather well now, he decided, and he felt some secret delight in the thought that he was doing everything with a certain flair.

Since he did not know Charity Cadwallader's phone number nor even her address, he was not sure when he would see her again. He felt certain it would be soon. He reasoned that it was Charity who had made all the moves. Why he had not seen that before, he would never know. He had been incredibly stupid about the whole business. He was naïve about women. He had never been able to figure them out, nor had he ever had much interest in the matter; but it was different now. He sipped Billy's Scotch and imagined his second meeting with Charity. They would dine at an expensive restaurant. He would remind the waiter to chill the Beaujolais. If he took her to that restaurant he had read about, which did not present a menu, he would not have to worry about stumbling over French or Italian. Everything would be served them. Over candlelight he would tell her about his business. He had so many ideas, good ones. Just this afternoon he had thought of an idea for a tie-in with a nonprofit organization like the Heart Fund. The organization could buy dollar autographs of famous people. Adam would have cards printed up which would say: *This autograph is a token gift. It symbolizes a $20 contribution to the Heart Fund made by (name of donor) in your name. Because you are the kind of person who would rather give than receive, this is your kind of gift.* . . . It was an idea that had everything—snob appeal, an attraction for a person's vanity, conscience, and benevolence. Adam could see endless possibilities in the idea. He had thought of a wonderful slogan to promote it: FOR THE PERSON WHO HAS EVERYTHING, INCLUDING A HEART. . . . He imagined Charity listening with a certain warm respect for him, as he told her about his idea. He imagined her writing to Billy, telling Billy what a fine person Adam was, not only kind and imaginative, but having a good business head as well. He was so delighted with this fantasy that he promptly made himself another drink, using two fingers of Scotch instead of one this time.

At nine o'clock, Adam was a little high. He had used up practically every background in his imagination, and in every candlelit restaurant, on every tree-lined walk, in all the various and fabulous places he had visited as he sat in Billy's deck divan, Charity had watched him with admiring eyes. He had been brilliant and dynamic; he had even been a bit amusing, which was rare for Adam. Charity wrote so many enthusiastic letters to Billy, that by nine, Billy was writing back, "Are you in love with Adam, or something?" . . . and Adam was laughing aloud. Let the neighbors think he was some kind of nut, he thought. He had never had a better time. His spirits were so buoyed by his daydreams that Adam had an uncontrollable desire to contact Charity that very night.

He went through everything of Billy's looking for her address. When this failed to produce any information, he decided on a direct course of action. She had told Adam she lived nearby. He parted his hair carefully before the hall mirror, slipped his suit coat on, and left the apartment whistling. "Another thing about Adam," Charity was writing Billy as Adam walked into the night; "he's so forceful."

At every apartment building where there was a doorman, Adam simply said: "What number apartment is the Cadwalladers', please? I'm expected."

He was continually told there were no Cadwalladers in the building.

Where there were no doormen, Adam read the nameplates on the bells.

He walked up and down Ninety-third Street and Ninety-second, and the block between on Park. When he came to Ninety-first Street, he started at Fifth and decided to work toward Madison. It was in this block that he came across them.

It was the boy he saw first. It was the piercing glint of the boy's thick glasses, caught in the streetlamp's light—the owlish look of the youngster. Adam saw him, and, once it registered that it was the same boy he had seen hanging on the garden fence of King School, he noticed the man and woman with him.

The woman wore dark glasses, though it was now past nine-thirty at night. Her hair was pulled back in an untidy bun, so that wisps of it strayed in the evening breeze, as though she had been hurrying and had not had time to secure it. It looked blond, or red—Adam could not be sure. A mink stole hung off her shoulders, again giving the appearance of slight dishevelment. She was a small woman, unusually thin. It seemed to Adam that she was frowning, though her face was half in the shadow. She held Timothy Schneider by the hand in a way which was not "holding hands," but more pulling him along, as though he were a heavy cart that held her back. The boy was looking behind himself at the man, holding his other hand out for the man to take. The man was a few paces away, and when he tried to take the boy's hand, the woman gave the boy another yank forward.

Adam was close to them then. It was then that he got his first glimpse of the man. Luther Schneider did not look at all as Adam had thought he would. He resembled the portrait on the cover of *Our Time* only vaguely. The features were the same, but there was something in his expression which Adam was surprised by. Adam could not remember ever having seen the single emotion of disappointment written on the face of a stranger, but he saw it on Luther Schneider's. It gave Adam a bewildering sensation, which manifested itself in an urge to break the woman's hold on the boy with his own hand.

If any of the threesome noticed Adam, they gave no

sign. As they passed, the woman was still edging ahead, pulling the boy. Adam heard her say: ". . . keep him up this late, not mine! Do you hear *me* making excuses for him? I gave that up long ago. Tiresome excuses!" Then she said something else Adam could not entirely hear, about never learning discipline.

Adam saw Luther Schneider sigh. It was a sigh of "giving up." Schneider was so tall as to make the woman look nearly comical by comparison, but there was nothing comical about the scene. He sighed, and then his shoulders seemed to relax in a slump. He fell back a few more paces, so the woman and boy were well ahead of him. Adam could hear the boy's high, nervous whine, as he was pulled along; then a shrill retort from the woman. Silence then, save for the groan of a bus starting on Fifth Avenue, and the clatter of the woman's heels.

Adam lighted a Gauloise and leaned against a chestnut tree near the curb. Mid-way in the block, by a street lamp, the woman turned in at a red brick house with a small spiral staircase leading up to it. With some difficulty, she yanked the boy with her. He caught the iron rail with his hand, letting his feet swing, to make it harder for her, but she jerked him away from it. A yellow door flashed open and shut. After a minute Luther Schneider turned in at the same house.

Adam tossed his Gauloise in the gutter. His search for Charity Cadwallader seemed suddenly pointless. The disappointment he had seen in the face of Luther Schneider was somehow contagious, for he suddenly felt a keen sense of disappointment himself. But at what? He walked toward Madison Avenue. He thought about the woman, and about the fact that he had never speculated at all as to what his own mother had been like. He had that one memory of her, but he had never built on it. His childhood fantasies of being like other boys never actually sketched a mother; only a father. He could not even recall anything very specific about Marshall Bollin's wife. She was simply Billy's mother, and he could not remember one conversation he had ever had with her, though there must have been many. Nearly all the employees and counselors of the Home were women, yet

Adam had forgotten half their names. Those whose names he did remember, he did not remember pleasantly.

At Madison and Ninety-third Street, Adam turned in at a bar. He ordered a double Scotch and sat far down at the end, away from the small congregation of people toward the front. Most of them had come into the bar alone, but they were talking back and forth the way they did in neighborhood bars. Let them, Adam thought; he even felt sorry for them. A bald, middle-aged man was saying very unfunny things at which they were all laughing uproariously. Adam put a quarter in the jukebox, forcing the bartender to turn down the sound on the television. The music helped drown out the laughter and the unfunny things the bald-headed man was saying. Adam had another double Scotch. The last thing Adam remembered clearly was taking off Billy's poodle cuff links and putting them down on the bar.

8

Geneva, Switzerland (WP) The four-year-old son of wealthy Doctor Thomas Zumbach was kidnapped from his home here last night. A note demanding a ransom of $100,000 was tied to the cord of the window shade in Thomas Zumbach, Jr.'s room. The Zumbachs' home is in Klatz, a small village on the outskirts of Geneva. Dr. and Mrs. Zumbach begged for police and public cooperation in being allowed to make a rendezvous with the kidnapper, in order to pay the ransom, and secure the safe return of their child.

Adam missed the poodle cufflinks as he was dressing Friday morning. On the Madison Avenue bus, with a blinding hangover, he tried to forget about it. When he read the story of the kidnapping in the *Times,* his eye caught the word "Klatz," and he was reminded of his carelessness all over again. That morning he had received an airmail postcard from Billy. Billy was staying in Klatz, commuting to the hospital in Geneva where his father was a patient.

Adam told himself the first thing he would do at the day's end would be to return to the bar where he had gotten so drunk last night. If the cuff links were not there, he would simply have to replace them, regardless of cost. He had no idea why he had taken them off in the first place. There were some dim recollections of talking to people in the bar, but they were too vague to explain anything. This morning, scrawled across a page in his Journal, he had found this notation: "Buy the Madison Avenue Inn and fire bartender!!!" He had scratched it out after he read it, and written under it: "Watch drinking!"

It was a steaming New York day, too hot and humid for mid-May. That fact, coupled with Adam's headache and stomach upset, made his work go rapidly and smoothly. Adam found that he was much better at business when he did not feel well, particularly if half of his difficulty was his own fault. By noon he had paid the piper more than his due. He had interviewed seven young men, and hired one to start as his helper in a week. He had concluded the lengthy correspondence on the Poe manuscript, and sent out four copies of the letter he had drafted yesterday, on the availability of the autograph albums. He had sorted the mail, made arrangements for a rare-coin concession to be added to The Mart, and talked at length with Geismar on the telephone. Geismar reiterated that he could not advance Adam anything against the inheritance, and Adam did not bother to enlighten him about the sale of "The Lucy Baker Album," the proceeds of which he could live on for some time.

Adam padlocked the door of The Mart at twelve-thirty. While he waited at the bar of the Villa D'Este, for a table, he called Dorothy Schackleford at her office. She was delighted with Adam's invitation for dinner, after Mrs. Auerbach's memorial service tomorrow night.

On the second Martini, Adam felt fine again. He or-

dered *suprême de volaille* for lunch, pointing to it so
that he did not have to attempt pronunciation of the
French. When the waiter repeated the order, Adam
made a phonetic spelling of it in his notebook, and when
it was served him, he wrote under the spelling, "breast
of chicken." For dessert, Adam had Cherries Jubilee,
coffee and a brandy. Over the brandy, he thought again
of Charity Cadwallader. He liked to remember her saying how she hated Billy. Now that he had Billy's address in Switzerland, he might even drop him a line and
hint at her feelings about him. He would not do it in a
brash way. He might simply say: "The other night when
Charity and I were having drinks, I tried to point out
that she was all wrong about you. Women are so stubborn! They often fail to see the real worth in a man." . . .
Something like that.

He ordered another brandy. What if he did write Billy
a letter like that, and his letter crossed with one of
Charity's? What if Charity wrote Billy that she hated
Adam? You couldn't trust women. . . . Why hadn't she
called to thank him for the roses and the pearl teardrop?
. . . The more Adam thought about the matter, the more
determined he felt to find out Charity's address immediately. He had to know where he stood. If she was going
to make a fool of him in Billy's eyes, he had to plan a
counterattack! He had a third brandy, smarting a bit
when the waiter presented the check along with it.

On his way back to Fifty-seventh Street, he felt himself weaving slightly. The Madison Avenue bus passed
him. For a fast second he thought he saw Charity looking out the window of the bus, looking and then laughing at him. He felt his face hot and red with embarrassment, and he made a great effort to walk in a straight
line. He could not be sure whether or not people were
laughing at him. When he tried to walk faster, he weaved
more. He felt sorry for himself. He had not had dinner
last night, and this morning his only breakfast had been
a glass of juice. No wonder the drinks had hit him. What
did the people who were laughing at him know about
his troubles? He could be physically ill, bereaved—anything; they would still laugh! He had always wanted to
protect Mrs. Auerbach from their laughter, but now

they were laughing at him. Who wanted to protect him? When he arrived at The Mart there were tears in his eyes.

At seven-thirty that night, Adam woke up on the couch back in the storeroom. He splashed water on his eyes, combed his hair, and locked up. In the street he bought an evening paper, and read more details on the kidnapping as he rode the Madison Avenue bus. There was a picture of the little boy. He had long curls and a round collar with a big black bow. His father, the newspaper reported, would pay *any* price for his safe return; it was his only child.

At Madison and Ninety-third, Adam got off the bus, and walked into the Madison Avenue Inn. There was a ballgame on the television, and only one man at the bar. The bartender was sitting on a stool, looking up at the television set. He did not look at Adam right away, but when he did, he spoke before Adam could.

"Well, well, well, Mr. Bollin," he said. "How are you this evening!"

It had been a long time since Adam had posed as Billy in a bar. He must have been *very* drunk last night, he thought, and he was glad that the bartender had given him that cue.

"I'm fine," he said. Then he explained that he had lost his cuff links, that he had remembered removing them there and putting them down on the bar.

The bartender said, "Oh, I remember too, Mr. Bollin."

"Well, may I have them back?" said Adam. "I hope they're here."

"They're here." The bartender was not smiling any more. His large hands were placed squarely on his hips. He was rocking back and forth on his heels, eyeing Adam coolly.

"I intend to have a drink," said Adam, "and I'd also like to have my cuff links back."

"I don't intend to serve you a drink, buddy!"

"I'm sorry if I was—out of hand last night . . . was I out of control or something?" The man at the end of the bar was not watching the ballgame now. He was looking at Adam. Adam decided to be as courteous as possible; it was the only way in such an embarrassing situation.

The bartender said, "I don't serve a fellow who's had too much to drink, buddy. I don't care what they offer me."

Adam tried to smile, but his mouth felt dry and tight. "I guess I offered you the cuff links . . . is that it?"

"That was *one* of your offers."

"I'm very sorry," said Adam. "I hadn't eaten, you see. My drinks hit me rather hard."

"A fellow with hundred dollar bills in his wallet ought to be able to buy himself a meal," the bartender said. He leaned on his elbows on the bar, watching Adam as though Adam were not all there.

Adam said, "I didn't have time to go to the bank yesterday. I had a very busy day. That's why I didn't get a chance to eat, you see. I didn't mean to be ostentatious."

The bartender said nothing, simply looked at him suspiciously.

Adam felt slightly irritated then. "If I bothered you, I'm sorry," he said. "I'll leave as soon as you give me my cuff links."

"I don't mind a guy who's had too much to drink," the bartender said. "I don't serve him, but he doesn't get my goat. You get my goat! Trying to throw big bills around is your business, buddy. The cuff links are another matter."

"Do I have to get a policeman?" said Adam.

The man at the end of the bar had moved down two stools. Adam began to be afraid.

"I wouldn't get a policeman if I were you, Mr. Bollin. That's your name, isn't it?"

"Yes, it is. And my initials are on my cuff links."

"Oh, I know that all right, buddy. I know something else too. I'm the one who ought to call the policeman. I just don't like any trouble, so I'm not going to call the policeman. You see, buddy," he said, leaning so close to Adam that Adam could smell onions on his breath, "this is what you might call a neighborhood bar! People in the neighborhood get to be pretty good friends, get to know each other, buddy. For instance, I know Mr. Bollin, and you ain't him!"

Adam was speechless. The man three stools away was staring at him, as was the bartender. The ballgame in the background was forgotten.

The bartender said, "Mr. Bollin has gone to Europe. He was in just last Saturday night. His old man is sick in Switzerland. You come in here last night and tell me you're Mr. Bollin, and you tell me you live where he lives. I'm not going to call any policeman, buddy, but you ain't getting Mr. Bollin's cuff links back. I'll just put them in a safe place for him, see, buddy? And if I were you, I'd pick some other guy to be. Some guy I don't know, buddy!"

Adam said, "Look, I'm a friend of Billy's, I—"

"I don't give a damn what you are, I don't like the looks of you! I met lots of Mr. Bollin's friends, and there's not a one like you! Not a one pretending he's someone he ain't either! Don't pull none of that stuff in *this* neighborhood! We all know our customers!"

The man at the bar said, "You need any help with him, Eddie?"

Adam did not wait to hear the bartender's answer. He turned and left the bar. He was perspiring through his suit.

The incident had its good results. Adam learned this as he munched a hamburger in The Soup Bowl three blocks away. Still shaken by the experience, so that his hands could hardly raise the coffee cup to his mouth, he had kept his head turned from the other people at the counter. His eyes focused on a florist shop at the corner of Ninety-sixth and Madison. He kept remembering how difficult it had been to find a florist in the neighborhood, that morning he had gone for eggs while Charity was at the apartment. He had finally found the one across the street from The Soup Bowl, the one he was looking at now. He had bought the bunch of violets there, and it occurred to him that Billy probably bought flowers at that florist's. He remembered the bartender saying that everyone in the neighborhood knew their customers.

Adam finished his hamburger and coffee, and headed

across the street. He straightened his tie, and smoothed his hair back before going into the florist's; then he asked for the owner. He introduced himself and explained that he was a friend of Mr. Bollin's. The florist's face broke into a wide grin, and he put his hand out to shake Adam's.

"I got a letter from Mr. Bollin only this morning," said Adam. He went on to say that Billy was staying in the same village where that dreadful kidnapping had occurred, and that Billy was visiting his father, who was ill in a Geneva hospital. The florist was gracious and smiling. He did not know Mr. Bollin's father was not well; he was so sorry to hear it; he would miss Mr. Bollin.

"Mr. Bollin wanted me to send flowers to a Miss Charity Cadwallader," Adam continued. "He wanted them to go out tonight. I'm afraid I left his letter at my office. I haven't any idea of the address."

Instantly the florist said, "Twenty-nine East Ninety-fourth. We do a lot of business with the Cadwalladers, too."

Adam suppressed a smile of victory. He ordered two dozen red and purple mixed anemones. On a card, he wrote: "If you don't call me at home tonight or at The Mart tomorrow morning, I'll call in person tomorrow night. Adam." He sealed the envelope while the florist assured him that delivery would be made that evening, before ten-thirty.

9

DANGER SIGNS IN HANDWRITING
1. *The circle i dot: this person resorts to attention-getting devices.*
2. *A break in the lower section of the letters a & o: dishonesty.*
3. *t bar slants downward: arrogance and cruelty.*
FROM ADAM BLESSING'S JOURNAL

On Saturday Adam did not open The Mart. The night before, near midnight, Charity Cadwallader called him. She agreed to meet Adam for cocktails and dinner. The call so elated Adam that he broke open a bottle of Billy's Nuits Saint-Georges. He sat drinking the wine until four in the morning. His mind seemed to swell with new ideas. He invented a game for adults that would teach them the calorie count in all foods. The winning of the game would depend partly on their knowledge of calories, partly on their knowledge of other nutritional information, and partly on chance. Adam believed it would sweep the country much as Monopoly had in the years after the depression, when money was foremost in people's mind. Health was the new concern. Adam called his game DO OR DIET. It was a penalty to DIET, a point to DO. He designed a simple board on which the game would be played. He planned to find a small manufacturer who would make up a lot of 100.

Another idea Adam got was for a way to promote the sale of autographs. He would place an unidentified autograph in The Mart's display windows on Fifty-seventh, with an analysis of the handwriting underneath. He would give several clues about the identity of the person, and offer a free handwriting analysis to anyone who could guess who it was. He might even offer a free handwriting analysis to anyone who made a purchase in The Mart. . . . One day, he would write an entire book on the psychology of handwriting.

The more wine he drank, the faster the ideas came. He had the money now to back his ideas, and there was something else. He had a new forcefulness, he felt. There was nothing he could not do now. He fell asleep in his clothes on Billy's couch and dreamed that he tracked down the kidnapper of the Zumbach boy, by analyzing the handwriting on the ransom note. Dr. Zumbach turned over the ransom money to him. Dr. Zumbach looked like the bartender in the Madison Avenue Inn. He apologized to Adam for not believing Adam was Billy Bollin.

It was not just his hangover that kept Adam from going to The Mart. He had overslept for one thing, but his real reason for staying home was that he wanted to clean the apartment. Charity was coming there that night for cocktails, before they dined out. Adam spent the entire afternoon cleaning, pausing only once at three-thirty, for a sandwich and a cold beer in the garden. It was then that he caught his third glimpse of Timothy Schneider.

He noticed the boy hanging on the fence, the same way he had first seen him. The boy was calling out the same thing: *"Regardez* Timmy Schneider," over and over. No one seemed to be paying any attention to him, but when a smaller boy wandered by, Timothy Schneider stuck out his foot and kicked him. The smaller boy screamed, and suddenly a man in a tweed suit yanked Timothy from the fence.

Adam heard the man say: "You feel hostile today, don't you, Tim?"

"I didn't hit him on purpose," the boy answered.

The man had him by the arm. "Oh yes, you did. Don't lie, Tim."

"I didn't see him!"

"Don't use that old excuse, Tim."

"I didn't see him! I didn't! I can't see everything!"

Adam set his bottle of beer down on the flagstone and leaned forward to watch the scene more closely. The Schneider boy was trying to pound the man's stomach with his fist. He kept repeating that he had not seen the boy he kicked. Finally, the man reached down and took the boy's thick glasses from his face. He held them in his hand.

The boy blinked and squinted, feeling the air around him with his fingers like a blind person.

"You only hit people when you can't see them, Tim," said the man. "So when you don't feel like hitting me any more, I'll return your glasses. You wouldn't hit me if you could see me, would you?"

The boy began to whimper. He reached for the fence and held on to it.

"You don't feel like hitting me now, do you?" the man said.

The boy shook his head from side to side, hanging to the fence with both hands.

The man said: "We all know you have bad eyesight, Tim, but don't use it as an excuse to be belligerent."

"I'm not belligerent!"

"You saw Robin. You kicked him deliberately."

The boy said nothing. He hung to the fence whimpering. The man in the tweeds walked over to him and put his arm around his shoulders. He gave the boy back his glasses. He said, "Will you apologize to Robin now?"

The boy nodded. He put his glasses on. Then he began to laugh.

"Laughing is good for you," the man said.

The boy shouted out *"Regardez* Timmy Schneider, Robin!" and he skipped wildly across the yard to shake the smaller boy's hand.

Adam finished his beer, thinking what a waste it was for a millionaire to have a son who was balmy. He remembered the disappointment in Luther Schneider's face. Adam wished he could think of an idea that Waverly Foods could use. Adam would call on Luther Schneider personally and present the idea. He imagined the scene, imagined Luther Schneider leaning back in a large leather swivel chair, a reflective expression on his face, his eyes watching Adam with growing interest.

"You say you got this idea yourself?" he would say.

Adam would nod modestly. He would have on a dark suit, with a fresh white shirt, and a quiet tie; his hair combed neatly, carefully parted, a half inch of clean white handkerchief showing from his pocket.

"Tell me about yourself," Luther Schneider would invite.

Adam's daydream was interrupted by the shrill sound of the ringing telephone. It was Geismar. Geismar wanted to know what Adam thought he was doing not keeping The Mart open. He was angry with Adam, and he made an unnecessary remark about Adam having retired a little prematurely. The call angered Adam, and when it was over, he made his first drink of the day—two fingers of whisky, neat.

By the time Charity arrived, Adam felt as good as he had late last night. He was impatient at the fact Charity wanted to discuss the kidnapping in Switzerland. Adam did not feel like talking about dreary situations or people he did not know. He wanted to talk about his new ideas.

In addition, it irritated him that Charity would not have a drink. It took away any festiveness. Adam himself was drinking double shots.

She sat across from him on Billy's conch-shaped couch. Several times Adam tried looking deeply into her very green eyes, but each time she lowered her lashes. She did not make the gesture shyly; she simply seemed disinterested in any sort of personal contact with Adam. Last night on the telephone she had said something about "settling everything for once and for all." After three strong whiskies, Adam 'interrupted her speculations about whether one or two people had kidnapped the Zumbach child.

"I want to ask you something," he said.

"Go right ahead." She sounded almost defiant; Adam could not figure her out.

"What did you mean about settling things? You said that last night."

"I wanted to thank you for the flowers and for the necklace," she said, "and I'm sorry you went to so much trouble."

"Why are you sorry?" Adam realized he was speaking in a loud voice. He interrupted her answer to apologize for it.

She said then, ". . . as I was saying, it's just been a mistake. I wanted to tell you that. And I know it was my fault."

Adam said, "I suppose Billy was such a good lover!" He got up and stomped into the kitchen, tipping the neck of the whisky bottle into his drink. Women were animals! He called out: "You said you hated Billy! Why did you hate him if he was such a great lover!"

She was behind him, on her feet with her bag and gloves in her hand. "Who mentioned Billy?" she said. "I didn't! I didn't say anything about anybody being a good lover, *or* a bad lover. You're drinking too much!"

"Does somebody only get one chance with you?" said Adam. He had a passing thought then that he did not even want another chance with her, not that way.

She walked over and touched the sleeve of his jacket. "Adam," she said, "it wasn't *that*. Believe me!"

"Oh, yes it was!" said Adam. "Billy's good and I'm rotten!"

"Let's forget about it, Adam. Let's go out and have a good dinner. Remember, we were going to dinner?"

"Where does Billy take you to dinner?" said Adam. "I might take you to the wrong place."

There was a soft look in Charity Cadwallader's eyes. They were so very green. Adam thought how he would like to just sit and look into her eyes, and have her look back at him—the way she had that first night at the Roosevelt. Everything was so complicated suddenly. She reached out and took the glass of whisky from his hand. "Come on, Adam," she said. "I'm hungry."

"Did you write Billy about me?" said Adam.

"Why do you care so much about Billy, Adam? Let's forget Billy for tonight. We'll just have a nice dinner somewhere."

"I hope you told him you came here and offered yourself," Adam said, "I hope you made *that* clear!"

She turned away from him abruptly and started toward the door. Adam caught her arm, holding it tightly. He felt himself choke up. He managed: "We're having dinner, aren't we?"

Charity looked closely at him; an unpleasant look. "You're not a very nice person, are you?" she said.

Adam felt tears start to sting his eyes. Even to himself his voice sounded infantile. "You said you'd have dinner with me—" self-pitying, mulish. He wished she would go; he wished she had never come at all. "Please!" he begged.

"Let go of my arm, Adam!"

"But you said—" Adam's voice broke. Tears began to run down his cheek. He let go of her arm. "Please—" and it was a sob. "It's so important," he whimpered.

"If we have dinner, Adam," she snapped at him, "I want to leave right now."

"My eyes," Adam whined, "they're all—"

"Splash cold water on your face!" said Charity Cadwallader.

They sat in one of the high-ceilinged back rooms of
Luchow's. Adam was amazed at how he had managed
to pull himself together, in the short while it had taken
them to cab there. Over a dark beer he told Charity he
had been under considerable strain these past few days.
He discussed his difficulties at The Mart with remarkable clarity, considering the fact that half of what he
discussed was a lie. Leaning back in the wooden chair,
smoking a Gauloise, he was himself again. He complimented Charity on her ability to use words of more than
two syllables, adding that he had never found this "in-
digenous" to young women. Adam had no idea whether
or not Charity did use words of more than two syllables,
but he knew that nearly everyone liked to hear it, and
almost no one thought they did not speak well. It was
delightful the way he was taking hold. He was able to
remember all the words from his own vocabulary list,
which he had painstakingly copied into his Journal each
week. He spoke with a delicious fluency, and he felt utterly controlled. Some of his German from his adult edu-
caton classes came back to him. He was able to say
Bitte to the waiter, and to point out to Charity that
Koenigsberger Klops were meat balls. Even the fact
that Charity told him she already knew that, did not
irritate Adam. He was invulnerable. Despite her objec-
tions, he had a second beer before ordering.

During the second beer, Adam got a marvellous idea.
Why didn't restaurants instead of having menus and
dozens of waiters, work out a master electronic selector?
It could operate the way a jukebox did. One could sit
at the table, punch "Sauerbraten" or "Alpenragout" and
have it recorded mechanically in the kitchen, at the
same time the price was tabulated automatically on a
check. Waiters would only be needed to serve the food.
Charity seemed impressed. At least she was quiet
and did not try to change the subject; she smiled and
enthused, and Adam had a third beer while he waited
for the wine list. He began to tell her all his ideas.

In the midst of his description of DO OR DIET, the
waiter brought the wine list. It annoyed Adam. Waiters

were always fast when you wanted them to be slow, and slow when you were in a hurry. Adam chose a Beaujolais, with instructions to chill it. He added an aside to Charity that Beaujolais and Swiss Dôle were the only red wines that could be profitably chilled. . . . Adam was continuing with his explanation of the game he had invented when he realized the waiter was lingering.

"Well?" said Adam.

"The lady is having Savannah Shad and you're having the duck?"

Adam nodded.

The waiter pointed out that a cold Moselle might be preferable.

Adam's heart began pounding.

"I think he's right, Adam," said Charity.

Then suddenly Adam regained his composure. Still, Adam was invulnerable; still he had hold. He very graciously instructed the waiter to bring whatever wine the waiter thought best. He used the word "indubitably;" indubitably the waiter knew wines better than Adam did. Charity was smiling and the waiter was smiling, and Adam began to smile too. He handed the wine list back with a flourish.

During dinner, Charity only played with her glass of wine. Adam no longer minded that she did not drink. It meant more for him, and he had the whole bottle, save for the tiny amount in her glass. He felt wildly happy and expansive. He said that tomorrow he was going to offer the Howard Johnson chain his idea for an electronic menu. He said he even knew a way to help finance the project, and the idea for this came as he talked. He would call on Luther Schneider, the head of Waverly Foods. A deal could be worked whereby Schneider would pay for the installation of the machine, if Howard Johnson's allowed Waverly to print across the machine's top that Waverly Foods were served. It would mean business for both, he told Charity, and as he told her this he realized he had not even finished his duck, and the bottle of wine was empty. He called for another beer then changed the order to another bottle of Moselle.

Charity was frowning slightly. Adam reassured her. It

was one of those nights when his liquor simply did not affect him.

"But let's talk about you!" he said. He leaned back, no longer interested in eating the rest of the duck. "What are your summer plans?"

"I'm going to Europe," she said. "Very soon."

It was a surprise to Adam, but on this fantastic evening nothing daunted him.

"I'll go along," he said. "Where will we go? Rome is a bore, so let's not go there."

She laughed. He did not like that laugh. He asked her what she was laughing at, and she said she was not laughing at anything. "I mean it," he said. He did, too. He would sell the *Stammbuch* tomorrow. He would let his helper run "The Mart" for the summer. It was his *Stammbuch*; it was his business, for that matter; he could do with The Mart what he pleased.

"Have you ever been to Europe, Adam?"

"Not because I couldn't afford to go," he said.

The waiter opened the second bottle of Moselle. Adam asked him if he had chilled it. The waiter smiled and nodded. Adam said to Charity: "Beaujolais and Swiss Dôle are the only red wines that can be profitably chilled."

"Don't you want some coffee, Adam?"

Adam said, "Certainly! *After* dinner!"

A party at the table opposite them were smiling. Adam smiled back, giving a smart little salute with his right hand.

Adam said, "In Europe we'll look Billy up! Won't *he* be surprised!"

"I dare say," said Charity. Then she said, "Adam, it's very late and I'm tired."

"Be glad you're a rich girl," said Adam. "You don't have to go to work tomorrow."

"Tomorrow's Sunday, Adam."

"All the more reason for celebrating," said Adam. "It's Saturday night."

As he said the words "Saturday night," something seemed to want to occur to Adam, but nothing did. He reached for the neck of the wine bottle and poured himself another glass. Some of the wine splashed onto the tablecloth.

Adam said, "It's the waiter's job to pour the wine. This fellow's not working very hard, is he?"

Suddenly Adam realized that Charity was calling the waiter.

"Look," Adam said, "I didn't mean to criticize him. I'm perfectly able to pour the wine. Let him alone. Let's talk about our trip! We might even start off at Klatz, hmmm?"

Charity persisted in calling the waiter. Adam was pleased that she was looking out for him, trying to please him. He said, "It's very nice of you, but maybe the fellow's had a hard day. Sunday's busy in Luchow's, and tomorrow's another new week. Let him be, Charity."

Adam sipped his wine. He liked the idea of starting off their European jaunt in Klatz. They could drive to Geneva and visit Marshall Bollin. Adam made a mental note to learn to drive a car before they sailed.

When the waiter finally appeared, he presented Charity with the check.

Adam said, "Good God, this fellow really *is* falling down on the job!" He reached across and took the check from the table.

Charity said, "Pay it, Adam. And then let's go!"

Adam couldn't blame her. A bad waiter could ruin everything. Adam hated to leave a half-full bottle of wine, but Charity was right. He should pay up and leave, and not bother to tip either. It did not have to mean the evening was over. They were very near Greenwich Village. They could go to some nice bar and have a brandy.

"I'll take care of everything," he smiled at Charity. "Don't let him upset you."

The waiter's handwriting was sloppy, and Adam had difficulty reading it. The *t* bars slanted downward and there were breaks in the lower sections of his *o*'s.

Adam said, "He's not only lazy, he's dishonest. You should see this writing, Charity."

"Never mind it, Adam, please. Let's go!"

"You're absolutely right," Adam said. Again the people at the opposite table smiled, and again Adam smiled back and gave another salute. They seemed to like him immensely. If the waiter had not been so irresponsible, Adam might well have asked them to join Charity and himself in a round of drinks.

When Adam reached for his wallet, it was gone. He searched all his pockets, twice. He said, "That does it!"

"Don't shout, Adam!"

"I don't mind a lazy waiter," said Adam, "but I'll not tolerate a thief!"

"Adam, please!"

Adam said, "He stole my wallet, Charity! I can't stand for that!"

"He didn't steal your wallet. You must have it."

"I don't! That's all there is to it!"

Charity looked angry. Again, Adam could not blame her. She said, "Wait a minute," and left the table. By rights, Adam knew he should go with her while she complained to the management, but he had a rather dizzy sensation. The wine was probably inferior, he decided. Bad whisky could do the same thing. He sampled a bit more of the wine. He felt so dizzy that he had to steady one hand with the other as he raised the glass to his lips. Some of the wine spilled onto his shirt. He saw the people at the next table watching him.

"Bad wine!" he called. "Poison! And my wallet stolen in the deal."

"Poor thing!" one of the women said to the man beside her. It was nice of the woman to sympathize. They were all nice people.

"Thank you," Adam cried out. "It's a good thing to know people care!"

He had more of the wine, holding it in his right hand, which was steadied by his right elbow leaning on the table. With his left hand he propped up his right arm, pushing the glass toward his mouth. Then the glass fell out of his hand, and the wine spilled all over his shirt, his suit, and the tablecloth. Another waiter—not his own —came hustling across the room.

"Ask my waiter to bring me another glass!" said Adam.

"If you'll come with me you can talk to your waiter," said the other waiter.

Adam shook his head from side to side with amazement. What kind of a place was it where the customers went to the waiters!

"Come on, sir!" the other waiter said. He had Adam's arm and he was actually trying to pull Adam to his feet. Adam felt very sad for the people at the next table. They would be treated the same way, no doubt, and they were nice people. Adam stood up, leaning against the other waiter.

"What kind of a place is this?" he said to the whole room. "You don't deserve this! Hang on to your wallets!"

The nice woman at the next table looked very sad. Adam wanted to comfort her. He tried to walk across to her, but the waiter pulled him back. Adam called to her: "Don't stay here! Look what's happening to me!"

Tears were suddenly streaming down his cheeks. They were all such nice people, all duped too. "Look at the handwriting," Adam said. He wanted to explain it, to tell them all to notice their waiters' handwritings, but he felt too tired now, and the waiter was stronger; the waiter was propelling him out of the room.

His own waiter was waiting at the EXIT with a man in a dark suit. The manager? . . . Adam pointed his finger at the man. "My wallet! I can't pay until the waiter gives it back."

"The lady has settled already, sir," said the man. "Good night, sir."

"The lady?" Adam said. What lady? The one at the next table who had smiled? Adam wanted to thank her, but the man in the dark suit had already opened the door, and Adam walked into the fresh air like a newly-freed prisoner.

"Here's the cab money she left for him," a voice said behind him.

Adam stood in the clean cool night. He saw his waiter out in the street trying to hail a taxi. He was making a get-away, Adam decided, and he had Adam's wallet with him. Adam began to cry again. Didn't anyone care that there were thieves loose in the world? He asked some of the people who passed him there on Fourteenth Street, but they only laughed, and the more they laughed, the more Adam wept.

10

Klatz, Switzerland

Dear Addie,

Father died last night. It came as a shock since he was doing so nicely when I left him yesterday afternoon. It was his desire to be buried wherever he died (you know how father hated fuss) so I am arranging a service for him in Geneva. Mother is flying here for it. There is no more to say on the subject, I guess. Please skip the usual sympathy note, since like father I agree that these things should pass with a minimum of ceremony.

What I am really writing to you about is Charity Cadwallader. You may have gathered that at one time Charity and I were rather close. I had intended to break off our relationship at the end of the summer, even before I left for Europe. Father's illness necessitated a sudden, and perhaps premature, break-up. I am fond of Charity, God knows, but we are two people who simply cannot "work things out." The suddenness of our very necessary split may prompt Charity to do something she would be sorry for later. I think she is quite hurt by the whole thing; even slightly antagonistic toward me. I do not expect you to understand this fully, since it is a most delicate and complicated involvement between two difficult people. However, I want to suggest that Charity might bring you into the matter as a way of getting even with me. She knows of our relationship as children, and she may misinterpret it to think I would be enraged were she to see you. Nothing could be more untrue. She can see whomever she pleases. However, it is only fair to warn you that her reasons for seeing you might have more to do with me than with you. . . . Don't take this the

76

wrong way, Addie. If I were in your situation, I would want to know the facts. Thus, my openness.

Charity has been seeing a psychoanalyst for years! I would not call her a bona fide neurotic, but neither is she a normal carefree young lady. She is a far cry from the girl you were with the night we all met, for example. She has none of that simplicity, nor any of that "above-board" honesty. In addition, she comes from a very good family, probably an overly-permissive family, which makes her a bit spoiled. But her family can trace their ancestry back to the Mayflower (no kidding either, Addie) and I hope you know what that means in terms of anyone they would accept as a proper young man for Charity. . . . I don't care about such things, but again—were I in your shoes, I would like to know the facts.

God knows I would be the last person to try and run down "Chary," but she is not what she seems to be. She is a very "mixed-up kid" who cannot use any more complications in her life. It is for this reason also that I ask you to consider all this. One of the many things I've always admired about you, Addie, is the fact you do not try to push in where you do not fit. Don't take that the wrong way. I mean it as a friend of long standing. I think very highly of you, or I would not have left you in my apartment where you have access to all my things.

I'll be here at least another ten days. The big news from here is the kidnapping, of course, but with father's illness and now his death, I have little time to be interested in anything else.

Yours,
Billy.

P.S. I am in need of my poodle-shaped cuff links. Be sure and insure them as they are very expensive.

Adam had no clothes on when he woke up Sunday noon. The thin Airmail Special was wadded up in his hand like a dirty tissue, so he did not pay it any attention right away. It had been pushed under his door last night. He had read it when he returned to Billy's apartment, but he did not remember it. He did not remember anything —not immediately. He lay on his stomach, his face in the pillow, his hands and wrists under the pillow. Columns of sunlight striped his back and his buttocks, and he could tell by the smell of everything that it was a very hot May day, no breeze and muggy.

It took him several long seconds to discover where he was and what day it was; then a few more such seconds to realize how he felt. Gradually, painfully, his memory began the play-back of last night. As far as it went, it was a faithful reproduction, but it ended with the waiter bringing a second bottle of wine. The rest was sketchy. His wallet had been stolen. Charity had complained to the management. A woman at the next table had paid the bill. He was not certain about any of it. He could not even remember taking Charity home, nor could he recall his arrival at Billy's. Here he was at any rate, so he must have seen her home, too; he had no recollection of an argument either. So far, so good.

A dream. Billy's father had died. Billy had told him to leave Charity alone. Or had Billy called him? A ringing phone seemed to stick in his memory; ringing, ringing, and he had not been able to pull himself from bed and answer it. . . . Was that right? He lay there thinking about it until his thirst became unbearable.

When he sat up, he saw his clothes strewn about the bedroom. Beside the night table, on one of the Etruscan chairs, was his wallet. He took that in at the same time he felt the wad of thin airmail paper balled up in his fist. His wallet had not been stolen after all, but he *distinctly* remembered . . . never mind. The letter next. Geneva postmark.

For twenty-five minutes he was sick in the bathroom. In between bouts of nausea, Adam sat on the top of the toilet cover, holding his head with his hands, his elbows propped on his knees. He could feel nothing about Marshall Bollin's death, only rage at Billy. In his mind he composed several letters to Billy. I'll-do-as-I-please letters and Who-do-you-think-you-are! letters. One of them said: "Of course I won't write you a sympathy note concerning your father. What a break for him to have you eternally out of his sight! I would rather write him a note of congratulations! . . . Another said that Charity Cadwallader, for all her "alleged" fabulous ancestry, had come to Adam offering her wares in the venerable tradition of any common whore. . . . After his sickness subsided, Adam got up and made himself an Alka-Seltzer. While he watched the bubbles, waiting for the tablets to dissolve, he composed another letter. Short, subtle, designed to infuriate Billy. In it he said he felt he could handle Charity; in fact, they would probably travel through Europe together this summer.

He did not even bother to dress. He sat naked at Billy's tambour desk, scratching the words across a piece of Billy's stationery, using Billy's quill pen. The phone interrupted him; a girl's voice. He did not recognize it.

"Yes, this is Adam. Who's this?"

"Eloise Siden, remember?"

"Eloise Siden . . . I think I remember."

"Dot's roomie."

Then he did remember. The girl from Texas who booked New York to Caracas and smelled of garlic.

"Oh, how are you?" said Adam.

"*I'm* fine, bub, but I can't say the same for Dot, thanks to you! Who in blue blazes do you think you are, bub! I suppose it's your idea of fun to stand someone up! First you get her to do your dirty work and show up at the confounded funeral service and then you hightail it off someplace else and don't even—"

God! Adam held the telephone arm away from his ear. He had completely forgotten the service for Mrs. Auerbach last night; forgotten his date for dinner afterward with Dorothy Schackleford!

"Listen!" he tried to interrupt Eloise Siden's bombardment, but he was glad that he could not, for he did not know what he would have said anyway. He was lower than a rat, said Eloise Siden, too low for worms to crawl under him. Eloise and Shirley Spriggs and Rose Marie Scoppettone and Norman had been up until all hours trying to quiet Dorothy down.

"Dotty said you must have been in an accident," Eloise Siden continued, "and she kept making us phone your place, but I knew the straight poop, bub! You never fooled me for a minute! Norman either! He'd like to plant one on your kisser good!"

Again, Adam held the telephone arm away. Shirley Spriggs, the girl in the Japanese kimona who had vowed not to dance for two years; and Rose Marie, whose last name meant "big gun" in Italian; who answered "*Mais oui*." Norman, fat bald slob Norman. . . . Adam could picture the whole affair. . . . Tomorrow he would call Dorothy Schackleford at her office. He would think of *some* explanation. He would take her to dinner at Ficklin's, the fancy restaurant without menus; he might even get theater tickets. It would be easy enough to straighten out the whole business where Dorothy Shackleford was concerned, but what about Geismar? Lately Geismar was sarcastic and suspicious, as though he were sitting in judgment. Adam knew Geismar had attended Mrs. Auerbach's service; Geismar was a goody-goody if Adam had ever seen one. Adam would have to invent an air-tight excuse for *that* one! He brought the phone back to his ear. Eloise Siden was calling him a two-faced turd. Adam hung up on her.

He finished the letter to Billy, addressed it and sealed the envelope. Tomorrow he would sell Goethe's son's *Stammbuch*. With part of the money he would replace what he had spent from the sale of "The Lucy Baker album." That would satisfy Geismar that Adam was doing nothing crooked. The *Stammbuch* was Adam's, after all; he did not have to wait for the will to be probated to sell something that was already his. With the rest of the money, Adam would go to Europe with Charity. He would still have enough left over to live on for years! . . . When he returned from Europe, he would re-open The Mart. He would remodel it, hire several helpers, and expand the business. He would marry Charity and invite Billy to be best man. He would name his first son after Billy. Oh, he would show Billy some tricks! Adam's spirits began to soar! His headache went and he began to feel marvellous. He would ask Billy to be his son's godfather. Adam laughed aloud. He even felt a certain affection for Billy at that moment. Life would become a game he would play with Billy. It was a fascinating idea. Perhaps Adam would one day write a novel about it—call it *The Eternal Contest*. It would be a best seller and Adam would dedicate it to Billy. Adam was so pleased with his reflections that he walked to the kitchen and made himself a Bloody Mary. Since he did not know Charity's telephone number, and it was not listed, the only choice Adam had was to call on her. He would do just that after his drink. He would shower and shave and dress in his new chalk-striped black wool worsted suit. If the florist was open on Sunday, he would buy a bouquet for Charity's mother. He drank the Bloody Mary, hoping that both Mr. and Mrs. Cadwallader would be at home. After all, he smiled to himself, he had to meet his future in-laws sometime, didn't he?

11

. . . and that in any event, Charity is leaving for Europe very soon. It behooves you to bear in mind that up until now, we have tolerated you in a manner which is completely out of proportion to the embarrassment and general harassment to which you have subjected us.

This past week has been one importunity after another. Your sober apologetics have been every bit as vulgar and distasteful as your inebriated demonstrations, and your primitive persistence is alarming. As I have pointed out to you more than once, Mr. Cadwallader is a cardiac. Not for that reason alone am I warning you now that any attempt at future contact with this family, will result in Police ac-

> *tion. None of us wants to see you or hear from you nor receive anything in the way of gifts, notes, letters or the like. I hope I make myself very clear, for there is no exception to the rule. One move on your part will mean my reporting you instantly!*
>
> *Sincerely,*
> VERA CAMERON CADWALLADER

It was Mrs. Cadwallader's letter that drove Adam to the Gracie Branch Post Office that Monday morning in June. He knew now that she really meant it. As he filled out the regulation change-of-address slip, he felt sad and sorry that he was forced to do something so under-handed. He wrote down Charity's name and address in the proper space, and then in the "changed to" space, he wrote Charity's name again, and "c/o William Bollin," with Billy's address following. In about two days, Adam would find Charity's mail in his box. Carefully, he signed Charity's name as she wrote it, the tightly-knotted *a*'s and all. The *a*'s meant that Charity was extremely secretive. That was another reason Adam had to go to such lengths.

Even though Adam had presented Charity with Billy's letter about her, Charity did not seem to realize that Billy was really against her! Once during Adam's calls on the Cadwalladers last week, Charity had even shouted that she loved Billy. Adam had been even more disheartened when Mrs. Cadwallader put in that Billy was a fine person, far more decent than Adam was. Either both of them were gullible beyond belief, or there was something Adam did not know. Adam had mulled it over in his mind throughout the long week end. Perhaps his own behavior had not been exactly exemplary; nonetheless it should be perfectly plain to the Cadwalladers that Adam thought more highly of Charity than did Billy. Adam had even tried to reason with Charity's mother, explaining to her that he would certainly never write in a letter that Charity was neurotic! In addition, Adam had pointed out that the Cadwalladers knew nothing at all about his character, and the fact that they were so against him from the start meant that Billy had been busy sabotaging Adam in some way.

Something was wrong somewhere; Adam knew it! An entire family simply did not turn on a young man without reason. He could appreciate the fact that they disapproved of Adam's appearances when he was not wholly sober—they were not drinking people; but Adam had never made "demonstrations" as Mrs. Cadwallader said he had. He had simply tried to reason with them. Only once had he leaned against the doorbell of their apartment after they had asked him to leave; and that time he had simply wanted to reassure Mr. Cadwallader that he was not interested in Charity because of her money. He had just wanted to say that, then leave, but they had made such an issue of it, even threatening to buzz the elevator and get help from the elevator man. It was shabby treatment all around. Maybe he was not Billy Bollin, he told them, but he was a human being with feelings just the same.

It surprised Adam that *Mrs.* Cadwallader had written the letter. She had seemed so nice in the beginning, trying to be polite, telling Adam he was a nice young man, but Charity simply was not interested in him. Adam explained that Charity had not even given him a chance, and a chance was all he wanted. Mrs. Cadwallader had acted as though she was sympathetic to him, but she told Adam there was nothing *she* could do. She could persuade Charity to see him, Adam pointed out. This she refused to do, and Adam was sure Billy was behind it. . . .

Charity herself Adam would never figure out. She told Adam that he had embarrassed her at Luchow's, but when Adam asked her how, she said there was no point in going into it. Adam tried to exact the evening's events from her, but she would not even show him the courtesy of sitting down with him and discussing it. What angered Adam most of all, and hurt him most deeply, was that Charity would not even make an appearance the last few times. Mr. Cadwallader said she was afraid of Adam, and Adam actually wept at that, right in front of Charity's parents. Billy again—he knew it! Anyone who knew Adam knew he would never lift a hand to a girl, never! Nor to any person! What did they think he was! He wept, and Mrs. Cadwallader added insult to injury by saying that Adam needed "help." Adam knew the kind of help she meant!

Of course he had apologized in a long letter. He had sent roses twice. When he attempted to send Mrs. Cadwallader a plant, toward the week's end, the florist told him in a thoroughly unpleasant manner, that the Cadwalladers were not accepting any more flowers from Adam.

Adam handed the change-of-address slip to the postal clerk.

"My sister asked me to drop this off," he said. "My sister's getting married to Mr. Bollin."

"Good for her!" said the clerk with a broad smile. Adam smiled back. The clerk was a nice fellow. There were some nice people left in the world after all.

On the way out of the post office, Adam rumpled the hair of a small boy in a playful gesture. He hoped the postal clerk noticed him doing it. There would be no reason for the clerk to be suspicious of him, but Adam liked to put in little touches. The clerk would think: pleasant young fellow, happy over his sister's marriage . . . He would file the change-of-address slip automatically.

When Adam did begin receiving Charity's mail, he was sure there would be a letter from Billy among the others, confirming Adam's suspicions that Billy was writing lies about Adam. Adam only wanted one scrap of evidence. When he got it, he would simply file another postal slip, re-routing Charity's mail back. If he was confronted with the same clerk, he would simply say that his sister was not marrying Mr. Bollin after all. He might even embellish the story a bit and say his sister had run off with a chap named Adam Blessing on the eve of her wedding. . . . Adam smiled and walked out into a cool spring's end day.

The Mart had been closed all last week. Geismar was furious with Adam, but Adam no longer cared what Geismar thought. Ever since their fight over his not having shown up for Mrs. Auerbach's service, Adam had made it clear that Geismar worked for him, and that he was not Adam's priest. Geismar called Adam "cold-blooded" and expressed some doubt at Adam's intentions to operate The Mart as Mrs. Auerbach had hoped he would. Adam told him that was none of his business.

Geismar would see what Adam would do with The Mart! Meanwhile, Adam had to concentrate on the present. He still had not located a buyer for the *Stammbuch*. He had filed for a passport, and he was already making inquiries with the steamship lines and airlines in an attempt to learn if Charity was booked yet. A surprise party, he explained, and while they were perfectly willing to try and help him, so far he had no information as to when she would go, or how.

Again, a letter to Charity from Billy might disclose details. Adam was only sorry he would never be able to tell Charity how he had found out any of the information that would be revealed, once he got his hands on a letter Billy wrote her. Charity would always believe that one of Billy's letters had been lost en route. Perhaps by the time she did discover it, she would not care a bit. In between then and now, Adam would convince her somehow that Billy was a very shallow person; that she had been totally wrong about Adam as well. He would follow her to the Orient, if necessary; in a thousand ways he would demonstrate to Charity Cadwallader that he, Adam, was the person she deserved. At some point afterwards, years away—the three of them might all be fast friends. Maybe then Adam would tell both of them about this very day and the trick at the post office. Adam imagined Billy's face, registering amazement at first, incredulity, then the break-through of laughter, the laughter of bygones-be-bygones. He could almost see Billy's head tossed back as he laughed, the shock of red hair bobbing, laughing and telling him he never would have guessed, and Charity laughing with them, the three like a happy family.

On Tuesday Adam had another fight with Geismar. Geismar said he rather imagined the State of New York would get everything Mrs. Auerbach had, if Adam did not knuckle down to business. They were going to need character witnesses and affidavits proving Adam's devotion to both Mrs. Auerbach and the business, said Geismar, and already too many merchants on the block with The Mart were aware it was not open lately. Adam explained that his helper would report at the week's end;

meanwhile Adam made arrangements to go to Washington, D.C. A dealer had expressed interest in the *Stammbuch*. Adam felt he could get the price he wanted for it, upwards of $30,000.

At four-forty-five Wednesday, Adam returned from his trip. After he got out of the cab and paid the driver, while he waited for his change, he saw King School letting out. He spotted Timothy Schneider immediately. The child was walking by himself, carrying a large briefcase, which he half-dragged along the sidewalk. A red sweater was tied about his waist, and he was dawdling as he walked, touching car fenders and walking with one leg in the gutter, one out. The sun made his glasses look like huge reflectors. On an impulse as he passed the boy, Adam said, "*Regardz* Timmy Schneider." He smiled at the boy when he said it, but the boy just stared after him, with his finger in his mouth, frowning. As Adam turned in, he looked back and saw the boy still staring, hanging to a parking-sign pole, the briefcase twirling in his hand. Adam had one second's thought about whether or not the boy should be loose like that, but he abandoned it when he opened his mailbox with his key. The letter from Billy was there. Mr. William Bollin to Miss Charity Cadwallader. Charity's address was inked out and Billy's New York address written to the side.

Adam dropped the rest of his mail into his coat pocket. He noticed a Special Delivery among some bills, and he hoped it was from the man in Washington making the sale definite. He recognized Geismar's handwriting on one envelope, and he saw a bill from the florist on the corner. There was also a bill from Saks, addressed to Charity and forwarded. Adam let himself in the apartment. He felt no compulsion to drop everything and rip open Billy's letter; quite the contrary. He wanted to enjoy it fully, savor it comfortably, out in the garden in the cool air. After he made himself a double Scotch on the rocks, he took the letter with him there. He took a swallow of the Scotch and began it:

My dearest Chary,

Father was buried and there was a very simple ceremony. I'm sorry I have not had much chance to write
since our talk on the phone. Believe me, I was not angry
(as you thought) because you called. It was what you
told me about Addie, and you going to call on him.
I know you were very guilty because of it, and in your
usual depression. I know you thought it would hurt me
or make me jealous (laughable in view of the fact it was
Addie), and I know you realize now that you were
wrong . . . That Chary, you were just involved in another of your neurotic schemes which never have
brought you any happiness.

I was angry on two counts. I was angry because I love
you in my way, and I hate to see you hurt yourself.
Also, I was angry that you ever brought Addie into the
matter. It was my own fault for introducing you to him
in the first place. Naturally you thought he was my
friend, particularly when I let him stay in my place.
The truth, of course, is that Addie is someone I pity.
That night we joined him and that girl I thought it might
make Addie feel important. I hadn't seen him in years,
and I didn't want to simply say hello and goodbye. Father's illness made it imperative for me to have someone
to stay in my place immediately. Addie seemed logical
enough. He's harmless and all that. . . . Normally,
though, I doubt that I'd even invite Addie for a drink at
my place. Not that's he an unbearable person . . . just
that he's always been rather silly. He was a terrible
pest in his younger years, with one of these asinine
"crushes" on my father. Poor father used to be so embarrassed by him, he would retreat at the sound of his
voice, stay locked in his study until Addie had finally
gone. I haven't kept track of Addie, but I suspect he's
something of a phony, pretends to be more than he is
and all that. For example, he told me he was part-owner
of that business. Later when he drank with me, the eve
of my departure, he told me he had hired some lawyer
the YMCA recommended to help probate his partner's
will. It just doesn't add up that a partner would not have
a lawyer of his own, if for no other reason than to le-
galize the partnership. Also, consulting the YMCA for a

lawyer isn't done by anyone very familiar with business and its ensuing responsibilities. It sounds fishy to me. I don't care, because who the hell is Addie to me! I just want to set you straight.

You say he's wearing my cuff links and my ties, also helping himself to my liquor. Let him. (Except for the cuff links. I know you hate them, but father gave them to me. I've already written him asking to have them returned. DON'T WORRY—I DIDN'T MENTION. ANYTHING ABOUT OUR CONVERSATION, OR EVEN THAT I KNEW YOU'D BEEN TO SEE HIM.) Nothing in my place is of great value that he could wear or drink. He's the petty-thief type, not a real threat to anyone or anything—so I'm not worried about that.

Enough about Addie. Just steer clear of him is my advice. He won't bother you; he's too much of a vegetable. About your plans to arrive here on Sunday the 17th. Chary, I can't promise you anything, much less that I'll even be here. This is to say that I don't want you to come. It will do neither of us any good. Believe me, Chary, it's better to leave things as they are. You know our problems. You know how miserable we make one another. I can't face it any more, and I know now nothing will ever improve between us. Chary, I hate to rub things in, but your conduct with Addie—that whole thing, is just more of the same, and for me, the last straw. Addie, of all people, too! Rather a goat!

It's your own business if you want to visit Europe, but count me out. If we happen to be in the same place at the same time, I suppose we're able to contain ourselves long enough to enjoy a drink together, but beyond that, Chary—no! With father's death I have increased responsibility and a great deal of business to attend to over here. Of all times, this is not the time for another lesson in how impossible it is for us to be with one another.

Weather fine, and mother under control. Hope you will finally learn that your impulsiveness only ends up in your misery. Don't come here, Chary. I don't want you to. It's done.

Billy.

Adam had begun crying at the point in the letter where Billy said he was a silly person. Now as he put the letter in the pocket of his shirt, his face was wet with tears. He wiped it with one of Billy's monogrammed handkerchiefs, which he took from his trousers, and he sat there letting more tears come, and wiping them away. He thought of how ironical it all was—of how only a few days before he had actually been looking forward to being friends with Billy, having him to his home—Charity's and his; and of the three of them laughing and reminiscing.

The fact that Charity had betrayed him did not sadden him as much as the way Billy wrote to her about him. Women were never to be counted on, but where were you when you could not count on a man you had grown up with? Adam went inside and reread the letter. He lay down on the bed and buried his face in the pillow. Now that he was free to sob as loudly and as much as he wanted, he found he could not. Perhaps he was sobbed out; he had been weeping more and more lately, the way he used to when he was much younger. It all went back to Billy. Adam rolled over on his back and lay wondering about this mysterious relationship between Charity and Billy. It sounded so intense to Adam. He could not imagine what it all involved. They were both play-acting, he decided; rich people who had nothing to do with their time but think about themselves. The more Adam pondered it, the more dejected he became, until finally he was in a very deep depression. He wondered if Charity had told Billy everything about that night, including the fact that Adam had been too drunk. He felt a sudden urge to simply get up, pack, and go back to the YMCA. Never think of either of them again . . . but in the next moment he saw himself bringing about a reconciliation between Charity and Billy, saw himself as the wise friend, listening thoughtfully to one and then the other, planning a dramatic and unexpected meeting of the pair. Charity and Billy would be face-to-face, alone. . . . All due to Adam, everything ironed out between them because of Adam's advice to each. Then the three of them would be great friends, with Charity and Billy always saying how it was Adam who had accomplished the whole thing; how it was dear Adam . . . dear Adam . . . Adam was in tears again. He got up and made himself a second drink, three fingers of Scotch, neat.

On the fourth drink, he remembered the rest of his mail. A florist bill for $132. A postcard from Dorothy Schackleford. It was mailed from Mystic, Connecticut. "Here for the day," it said. "Driving back tonight. Norman and me. We ate at this restaurant. $6 for a lobster but worth it. Am not mad at you any longer. Forgive and forget, my motto! Love, Dotty." In the envelope from Geismar there was simply a bill for $50, with a notation on a typewriter: "for services rendered." Under it Geismar had written: "Under the circumstances this is just for minimum expenses." Geismar had quit, was that it? Adam shrugged. Let him, he thought. He poured another shot of Scotch and opened the Special Delivery.

Dear Mr. Blessing:

I will be here at the Commodore Hotel for three days more before I move into a new apartment. You may contact me here. Mr. Geismar informs me you are in Washington, but are expected back any day. I will appreciate your getting in touch with me immediately. I just read of my sister's death in a Denver paper three days ago.

Foremost in my mind is the return of the *Stammbuck* of Goethe's son, which my sister had always promised to my own boy. We are not interested in selling it, so if you are involved in any such negotiations, please cancel them.

In going over things today at The Mart, I notice an book called "The Lucy Baker Album" was sold for $1500, since my sister's death. You must have the bankbooks with this amount deposited, and I would appreciate having them—any that you are holding. The business and the inventory will be put on auction in August, but I will not need any assistance in this matter or in any concerning the business, as I have arranged for that elsewhere.

My sister and I stopped corresponding about a year ago, but up until then we corresponded several times a year. I do not remember her ever mentioning you, Mr. Blessing. However, I am sure you are reliable and I can count on you without having to put undue pressure on you. I am quite concerned about the *Stammbuch* and the Lucy Baker money. Please call at once.

Sincerely,
Ida Gottlieb Vickerstaff

Adam was drunk when Geismar called an hour later.

"There was always a chance an unknown relative would show up, Adam. She's a reasonable person. If you've spent some of the Lucy Baker money, she'll let you pay her back gradually."

Adam managed to say, "But the *Stammbuch* is mine! It's my *Stammbuch!*"

"Look, Adam," said Geismar. "The bubble's a bust. That's all."

"Bubble," Adam repeated to himself. He seemed to see many bubbles then, bubbles that danced in the pink glass of Chiaretto del Garda which Adam held in his hand. Each bubble had a face—Billy's. Adam set the glass on the table by the telephone and tried to bust the bubbles with his fingers. It only made Billy's faces laugh and fizz.

"Good night Adam," the telephone said.

Adam put the phone's arm in the pocket of his trousers. He picked up the neck of the wine bottle and poured more wine over the bubbles, until the bubbles spilled over and dribbled along the table and died on the rug.

"Good night, Billy," said Adam. He lay down on the rug with his cheek caressing the dampness. It was cool. He passed out, smiling.

Epilogue

From *New York World*—

TIMMY IS SAFE!

June 13 (W.P.)—Nine-year-old Timmy Schneider is safe. He is confused and sleepy, and he does not have his eyeglasses, without which he sees very little, but he is safe.

Kidnapped from somewhere between King School and the Schneider home, on an afternoon three days ago, young Timmy was not able to enlighten authorities on his experience, other than to say this: "A man bumped into me and my glasses fell off. There was a crunch and the man said they were broken. He said he knew me and had come to take me home, but first he said we would get them fixed. I told him I had a pair at home if he would take me there, but he said my father was waiting for me, and we would fix my glasses on the way. He called me Timmy and asked me where my big briefcase was, and he teased me about it. We laughed a lot. We took a bus a long way, I think, crosstown, uptown, I'm not sure. He took me to an apartment and a dark room. There were no sheets on the bed, and no furniture but a bed. I slept a lot. He gave me aspirin and it made me sleepy. I think I spent a few nights there. I woke up here, that's all I remember."

"Here" was the lobby of King School. Timmy was found there this morning at ten-thirty, by painters who are redecorating. The school closed for the summer the day after Timmy was abducted. Timmy was found curled up in the vestibule. He had no recollection of how he got there, but the painters say he was not there at seven-thirty when they reported. King School is a private school for "special" children.

Between the time Timmy was kidnapped and returned, Luther Van den Perre Schneider paid a ransom estimated to be $100,000. How it was paid, where it was paid—these details are known only by Schneider and the kidnapper. Throughout the ordeal it was Schneider's wish to keep authorities out of the affair. Schneider expressed "complete confidence" in the kidnapper of his child, saying he believed that once the money was turned over, his boy would be returned safely. Schneider's five words, "I have faith in him," will perhaps go down in criminal history as one of the ironies of the human spirit. There seemed to be almost a mystical character to Schneider's conviction that the kidnapper would abide by the pact he had set up with the boy's father. In the ranson note the kidnapper had said: "I need the money as you need the boy. You do this for me, and I will not fail you, sir." The whole atmosphere of this case was that of a "gentleman's agreement." Once Schneider appeared at King School to claim his boy, he refused to discuss any details. He seemed angry that reporters had questioned his son, and he stopped the boy from describing the man who had held him captive. Timmy Schneider had gotten only so far in his description, only far enough to identify his captor as a "thin" person. Schneider interrupted his son, and explained to reporters that Timmy, without his glasses, saw only shadows. "He can tell you nothing!" Schneider snapped. "And I won't discuss this matter ever."

"Gentleman's agreement" or no, there was some speculation at whether or not the kidnapper had threatened Schneider with further violence to Timmy, if Schneider gave him away in any detail. Police were nearly enraged at the wealthy manufacturer, president of Waverly Foods, for his total lack of cooperation with them. Schneider's wife, the former Win Griswold, one-time society beauty, was the one to report the kidnapping, and to give the few details police had. She subsequently broke down, and was unavailable to anyone but members of the family. Schneider explained she had been very ill this past year.

This was the second major kidnapping in two months. The first was that of Dr. Thomas Zumbach's son in Klatz, Switzerland. Thomas Zumbach, Jr., age 4, was found choked to death in a woods between Geneva and Klatz, shortly after Zumbach had made arrangements to pay the ransom. The kidnapper was apparently frightened by police who had trailed Zumbach to a rendezvous spot. The kidnapper did not show up, and the boy was found nearby. Police working on the Schneider case felt the facts of the Zumbach case influenced Schneider to work independently of them.

A doctor who examined Timmy said the boy had been fed pills of some sort, undoubtedly tranquillizers or sedatives. The nearly-empty bedroom the boy described, and the mattress without sheets, led authorities to believe the kidnapper had perhaps rented a place especially for this purpose. Police were checking with apartment-house superintendents.

PART TWO

12

> *". . . and I often think of Timmy, too, and see him
> asleep on Billy's mattress, afternoons when I would
> sit there in the dark and watch him. I suppose one
> of my smartest moves was to strip Billy's bedroom
> of rugs, furniture and blankets during those few days
> when Tim was my guest, but I wish I had been able
> to make him more comfortable. It does not seem
> that a year has passed. Too much of it was spent
> in Bidart! Ah well—"*
>
> FROM ADAM BLESSING'S JOURNAL

He was huskier now, not quite "plump." He saw his reflection in the window of the small café, as he nursed an aperitif before lunch, at an outside table. His hair was no longer parted and cut short, but thick now, combed straight back with an almost pompadour effect, and longer than he wore it back home. He had grown a beard, too. In Europe no one looked twice at a man with a beard. Adam liked his—it gave him a certain dignity. To his surprise and delight, it had grown in darker than his hair, and the contrast was interesting. White-blond hair, nearly black beard, and his face was tanned from a spring of warm sun, spent in southern France. His jowls were a bit flabby, and his cheeks had filled out more than he liked, but he could blame that on the wretched starches the hospital had served continually. He was glad to be away from there; glad to be back in Paris. His breakdown had occurred in late January. One morning he had awakened in his room at the Quai Voltaire, to discover he had forgotten how to tie his shoes. A psychiatrist told him of the "rest" villa for overwrought businessmen, in southern France. It was located in a sleepy Basque village called Bidart. A total of five months Adam had spent there.

He ordered another Cassegrain. The restaurant was famous for this aperitif—a glass of Montrachet colored by a drop of black currant liquor from Dijon. In the months before his breakdown, he had come here often. He needed the stronger stuff in those days; no aperitifs about it. Now it was moderation in all things. Adam smiled, remembering Dr. Melnik's advice: "Moderation in everything, Adam; moderation in moderation, too."

A feeling of bitterness followed the smile. He had almost begun to trust Melnik; he had nearly believed they were friends. During the months Adam had been there for recuperation, Melnik had become fascinated with Adam's handwriting analyses. For his own amusement, Adam had done analyses of his fellow patients. Most everyone had looked upon it as a form of "fortune-telling," more than character reading; few had taken it seriously. It was considered great "fun." Melnik knew better. He had studied graphology in Zürich, and he congratulated Adam on his remarkable intuitiveness. When Adam was practically recovered, Melnik often invited him to his quarters for dinner. Together they would discuss this one and that one, and Melnik would listen to what Adam had to say, as though Adam were a colleague. It had inspired him to work harder at his system, to improvise and add to his theories with a seriousness he had never had before. He felt useful and important, and before long many patients were good-naturedly calling Adam, Dr. Blessing.

A month or so before he was ready to leave, Adam went to Melnik with an offer. He would stay on as staff. He did not care about a title nor a salary. It was a place for him. He would even do menial work as well. Melnik refused the offer.

"Many patients," said Melnik, "think they want to stay on here after they're well. They offer to empty bed-pans for the privilege. But the most important part of getting well, Adam, is leaving."

Adam had been hurt at being classed with all the others.

"Then you were just flattering me, after all. The same as you would praise someone's idiotic finger-painting!"

Melnik had frowned: "If you start thinking that way again, you'll get sick again."

So Adam had been cast out again. Again, he was on his own.

The waiter served him sweetbreads with truffles, and Adam resisted a temptation to wash it down with a bottle of fine wine. He had discovered that if he read along with his meals, he did not miss the wine nearly as much. He unfolded a copy of the Paris *Tribune,* and spread it out beside his plate. As he read the theater ads, he thought of his newest idea, which he had dreamed up on the train from Biarritz. Since Adam had been in Europe, the theater had become his main sober distraction. On the train from Biarritz, he had been looking forward to the theater again, after so long an exile. He had pictured himself standing in the familiar line for tickets. Then, it had come to him—his idea. There ought to be an electronic ticket machine which could be installed in hotels, restaurants, department stores—in places all over the country. One could buy tickets to the various hits by consulting the availabilities which would be registered on the machines. Halfway to Paris he had taken his pocket dictionary out and begun composing a letter. In it, he informed a likely manufacturer that he himself would invest a considerable sum in the project. . . . The letter, unfinished, was still in Adam's bag at the hotel. Maybe, Adam mused, he would really get busy on *this* idea. Melnik had told him it was essential that he get busy.

Adam read on in the *Tribune,* half of his mind mulling over the possibility that Melnik might be actually jealous of him. After all, Melnik worked hard for very little money, and it was no secret to Melnik that Adam had plenty. Adam had told him the same story he told everyone else: that he had inherited money and realized handsome gains from wise investments.

Adam had not yet made any investments. Part of the reason was that he did not trust a broker, and he was never without fear that such a transaction might cast suspicion on him. He had no knowledge whether large investments were reported to the police; it seemed anything was likely so long as the authorities were searching for him. Adam was convinced by now that Schneider had kept his word; he had not marked the ransom money. Adam hoped to invest the money some way, to perhaps interest a manufacturer in one of his own ideas, to ultimately double the amount remaining. It was his dream to repay Schneider. He had paid back Mrs. Auerbach's sister for the Lucy Baker money gradually, so as not to be suspect. The day after he had returned Timmy, Adam had taken a job in Macy's, and stuck it out three months. He had told Dorothy Schackleford the *Stammbuch* was his, and he was working at the Macy's job until he could arrange for the *Stammbuch's* sale. Each pay day he gave Mrs. Auerbach's sister $60, so that at the end of three months, moved by his earnest endeavors to make up the money, she dropped the remainder of the debt. He was free then to go to Europe; certain, by then, the money was unmarked; out-of-debt, and clear. . . . Adam never liked to think of his money as "the ransom money." It was "the loan" in his mind. He felt a nearly ethereal tie with Luther Schneider, every bit as strong as a blood tie. During their one telephone conversation, when Adam had arranged for Schneider to leave the money in King School's outside trash cans, Schneider had said: "I keep my promises. I know you keep yours, too. I believe in you. Remember that." No one had ever said such a very touching, kind thing to Adam Blessing. He would make it up to Luther Schneider someday, somehow.

Last Christmas from Biarritz, Adam had sent a model of a tiny Basque fishing boat to Timmy Schneider. He had so much wanted to sign his name to a card and enclose it. Perhaps Luther Schneider would never guess who "Adam Blessing" was—Schneider had so many business involvements all over the world; it could be just someone he had forgotten. Yet what if he did suspect who Adam Blessing was? Adam liked the idea of Schneider knowing his name, knowing that at Christmas he had remembered Timmy. He wanted, in some way, to tell

Schneider that he was not just a crook, not just some-one who did not care . . . In the end, he chose not to in-clude a card. He would remain anonymous until he could come face-to-face with Luther Schneider, hand him a check for the full amount of "the loan," thank him, and then perhaps invite Schneider to have a drink with him. He would honestly like to know Schneider better. He would like to tell Schneider how he had managed to double the money; win his respect and admiration. . . . Last Christmas Adam had been so very lonely. . . . He had thought of Luther Schneider often.

Midway through the sweetbreads, Adam decided to buy a gift for Schneider after lunch. Adam was not a stranger to the man's tastes and habits. Those three months in New York last summer, Adam had visited many back-number magazine stores. There was the por-trait in *Town and County* on Schneider; the piece in *Fortune,* and the cover story in *Our Time*. In addition, all the newspapers had been filled with stories on Schnei-der and his family, during the kidnapping period. Adam had pored through them.

While Adam was "resting" in Bidart, he had read a few books on silver. Luther Schneider was an avid silver collector. Adam would find him something special—a Sheffield-plate egg stand, perhaps, or one of those rare, helmet-shaped silver cream jugs. It would be something interesting for Adam to do with his afternoon. He was tired of going to the movies, and tired of listening to his French and Italian language records back in his hotel room, tired, as well, of his immense loneliness. It had been the latter that had gotten him into so much trouble before his breakdown. He had done remarkably well about his drinking during the three months in New York last summer. Loneliness had never really plagued Adam until his arrival in Europe; then he had needed to drink to forget it. No more of that. In Bidart he had made up his mind that upon his return to Paris he would get things under control; start doing constructive things about his ideas. He liked the idea of buying Schneider the gift, as a sort of symbolic token of a turning-point. From now on he would work to repay Schneider. Adam was pleased with the thought. Euphoria began to creep in. Still—he did not order the wine his meal so dearly lacked. Indeed, a turning-point. He smiled and turned the page of his newspaper, and then he came upon the short notice in the *Tribune*'s "Americans in Paris" column.

It was a single-line entry: "Mrs. Vera Cameron Cadwallader of New York City is staying at the Hotel Continental."

At six-thirty that evening Vera Cameron Cadwallader was waiting for him in the Continental's Cour d'Honneur. She was sitting at a table under one of the red-and-white striped umbrellas. In the note which Adam had dropped off at the hotel that afternoon, he had simply said that he was a friend of Charity's; that he would very much enjoy having a cocktail with her. He put an undecipherable signature at the end, and arrived a few minutes later than the appointed time, for fear she would see him and refuse to join him.

Adam sat down. "You don't remember me?"

She seemed anxious to please, but suspicious. She did not remember him at all; the beard, the extra weight— Adam supposed she was thinking that Charity did not know anyone who wore a beard. She smiled. "I'm sorry. Your name—I can't think of it, and on your note I couldn't make it out."

"First of all, I've changed a great deal," said Adam, "not just in appearance, Mrs. Cadwallader. I want you to understand that before I go on any further. I'm a different—"

"Blessing," she said then. "You're that Adam Blessing."

"Not *that* Adam Blessing, Mrs. Cadwallader, I assure you. You were so very right when you made the remark that I needed help, remember?"

She was looking down at her white gloves, playing with the fingers nervously. "I don't remember."

"Please just give me a few minutes to talk with you."

"Of course," she said. She did not look across at him. She sipped her aperitif, still occupied with the gloves.

"I was an awful fool, but that's all changed now. I was in the midst of a nervous breakdown."

"I'm sorry," she said.

"I make you nervous, don't I? I don't want to. I have great admiration for you."

"How long," she said looking at him then, "are you going to be in Paris?"

Adam knew she meant to keep the conversation as impersonal as possible.

"I live here now," he said.

"How nice for you."

"And Charity? How's Charity?" He did not mean to say her name so soon after the conversation had begun, but Mrs. Cadwallader's nervousness was contagious.

"Very happy," she said.

"I heard they were abroad. I thought you might all be traveling together." It was a shot in the dark. He had no idea where Billy and Charity were.

"No, they're in Rome," she said.

"I thought Billy was bored with Rome. I thought he hated Rome!" He told himself to go easy; the old tone was back in his voice, the breathless feeling. He saw Mrs. Cadwallader look more closely at him, and he laughed. "It's a joke Billy and I had," he said. "I used to kid with Billy about Rome."

"What about Rome?"

"Just a joke Billy and I had," said Adam.

"I don't understand."

"Oh, well, it's not important. I—I don't even know how it came up." There was silence. Adam wanted to signal for the waiter, but he was afraid that it would simply give her an excuse to say she could not join him in the drink, an excuse to pay for her own drink and leave. Adam said, "It's lovely here, isn't it?"

"Yes, lovely."

"I was very happy when I read of their marriage last summer." He coughed, to camouflage his shortness of breath. "It must have been very romantic, eloping that way, spur of the moment and all."

"Yes."

"I read about it in the newspaper," said Adam. "I read about it just a week before I left for Europe. I'd hoped to run into them, but we were never in the same places, it seems." In Venice, though, I came close, Adam thought grimly; missed them there by two days.

"Are you working over here, Mr. Blessing?"

"I'm hunting down some rare silver pieces for a New York collector," said Adam. "It's very interesting . . . I suppose Billy is working for his father's firm. I mean, he took it over, didn't he?"

"Yes."

"Yes, I thought so. I thought it would be something like that." Adam's voice was husky, his throat very dry. Out of the corner of his eyes, he could see the waiter, but he did not chance signaling him. Mrs. Cadwallader had nearly finished her aperitif.

"How's Mr. Cadwallader?" said Adam.

"He passed on at Christmas time."

"I'm sorry."

"Mr. Blessing, I have a dinner engagement and—"

"I know I said the wrong thing. I should have kept up on things more," said Adam, "but it's hard over here. I'm sorry about Mr. Cadwallader's death. I know it must be hard. I don't mean to keep saying the word "hard." I guess sometimes life just seems that way. I wish you wouldn't leave just yet, Mrs. Cadwallader. I thought we might have one drink together." The words rushed out of him, and Mrs. Cadwallader seemed to be looking at him as though he were very strange.

Adam said, "Please . . . I mean—I was in love with Charity." That, he had never intended to say either.

Mrs. Cadwallader stiffened and took her gloves from the table, placing them in her lap. "I have a dinner engagement," she repeated. "Young man, you hardly knew Charity. It's something you made more of than the situation warranted. Now, I'm very sorry, but there's nothing I can do."

The old symptoms were returning. The feeling of wanting to cry.

Adam said, "Their marriage was my fault."

"You don't know what you're talking about Mr. Blessing." She tried to catch the waiter's eye with a raised finger, but the waiter hurried off in another direction. She opened her purse.

Adam said, "Billy didn't even want her to join him. She went without even knowing that, Mrs. Cadwallader. I was busy trying to get enough money together to go after her and bring her back, but I didn't have time."

"Mr. Blessing, Charity and Billy are very happy." She was taking out bills from a large foreign billfold.

"Doesn't it mean anything to you that Billy never intended her to join him? He wanted to call off the whole thing, Mrs. Cadwallader. I can't tell you how I know that but—"

She interrupted him. "I'm sorry, Mr. Blessing," placing the francs on the table, rising, "I must go now."

Adam rose and went alongside her. "It's my fault, the whole thing," he said, "and you don't know what I've been through. I wish you knew! Even after their marriage, I was ready to help Charity, take her back home. I tried to find them. Sometimes I just went from city to city looking for them and—"

Mrs. Cadwallader stopped at the exit of the Cour d'Honneur. "Mr. Blessing," she said, "I want you to leave my company. I will report you if you don't. You are a very ill person, in my opinion."

"Not any more, Mrs. Cadwallader! Believe me, I *had* my breakdown! I was in southern France, in a town called Bidart at a hospital. You can call Dr. Melnik there! Ask him!"

She was walking away from him.

"Dr. Andre Melnik!" Adam called after her. "Write him, Mrs. Cadwallader!"

People were staring at Adam. He knew his face was very red, perspiring. He tried to get his breath. He saw Mrs. Cadwallader stop a uniformed employee of the hotel, speak with him momentarily, turn and point Adam out.

Adam hurried through the archway, along the stone sidewalk to the Rue de Castiglione. Once in the street, he lighted a Gauloise and leaned against a pillar until he could stop shaking. Over and over as he stood there, he tried to convince himself that this is where it should end. That part of his life was all over, wasn't it? He was well now; and if it had seemed for those few moments in the Cour d'Honneur, to be starting up again, well, then—let it end again.

But like all the other endings, it was a beginning. Adam realized this. He drew a deep breath, let it out, gave in. There you have it—he was glad, too. He looked forward to what he knew was ahead of him. A little chill of excitement ran through him. Packing again, it would mean, and consulting the train schedules; then the embarkation, with its sweet, nervous anticipation; and the journey itself, too tense to read or sleep or think of anything all through it but the journey's end . . . the inevitable round of hotels, the inquiries, the coming closer and closer. . . . This time though he was ahead of the game, for he knew positively that Billy was in Rome.

"What is it you really want from him? Or her?" Melnik used to ask.

And it used to stump Adam. He could never answer Melnik, and soon there was no need any longer for Melnik to ask. Now, the answer was so simple Adam began to grin as he thought about it. He did not want anything *from* them—of course, that was a silly way of putting it, and damn Melnik for that! Adam simply wanted to be with them, to help them, too. Why had he never thought to put it that way to Melnik?

Adam tossed the Gauloise to the gutter with a flick of his finger, and with a new, but very familiar spring to his step, he started off.

13

The Bartender
Madison Avenue Inn,
Madison and 93rd
New York, New York
U.S.A.

You don't remember me, probably, but once you put me out. I'm Billy Bollin's friend. I bear you no ill will and send this as a token of my good wishes. Adam B.

POSTCARD FROM PARIS MAILED IN JANUARY

Adam checked first with the Grand, then the Excelsior when he arrived in Rome, and on his third try—the Mediterraneo—he located them. They were not in. Adam left a note for them saying he would be by at six o'clock. Then he set out to find himself a place to stay. Because it was June and the height of the tourist season, it was not easy, but shortly after two in the afternoon, he found a room at the Delle Nazioni. He spent a few hours loafing about in his room, waiting for the stores to open. The last time he had been in Rome, sometime in early October, he had not understood about the stores staying closed between one and three or four in the afternoon. It was an unhappy memory, and an unhappy period. He had gone to Rome on the chance he might find them yet, though he knew Billy disliked Rome. He had gone everywhere that fall on chance, and each failure brought on a brief bout of drinking, which invariably delayed his departure. In Rome he had suffered through one of his most extended binges, starting at breakfast usually, so that by lunchtime he was already drunk enough to be laughed at. He remembered one afternoon on the Via Francesco Crispi, pulling on the iron gate that locked a small handicraft shop, begging to be let in at the top of his lungs. Somehow he had thought the shopowners were against him in particular, that they had been warned (perhaps by the proprietor of the café where he had lunched) that he was coming in their direction. A nasty scene ensued, with police dragging him away, passers-by gaping and snickering at him. He had left Rome the very next day, vowing he would never return to face such humiliation again.

Adam realized now that all of the trouble last fall and winter had been his own fault. A breakdown, Melnik had termed it. Adam had wished he could tell Melnik the reasons for it, the tension he had suffered through, the fear that any moment the authorities would find him out. A lot of businessmen, said Melnik, can't take the pressure any longer, crack under it. . . . Stop reading the stock quotations, said Melnik . . . rest awhile and work on "the other thing" . . . Billy was the other thing. A business rival, Adam had explained, married the woman I wanted to marry, without even loving her. . . . Melnik's advice was to accept the fact of the marriage. What was the word Melnik used? Scotomise . . . Don't scotomise it . . . Well, Adam did not intend to scotomise it. He simply intended to be sure everything was all right with them. It was Adam's fault Charity had never received the letter Billy wrote her, telling her not to join him in Switzerland. That much he owed them, anyway—to be sure that everything was all right.

Around four o'clock, Adam walked in the oppressive summer heat to the Via Condotti. At number 84, he bought a handsome foulard and damask tie-silk dressing gown, explaining that he wished it gift-wrapped. A wedding gift for Billy, if they were still determined to carry on with their marriage. Otherwise Adam would keep it for himself. From the Via Condotti, Adam went to Via Frattina. At Myricae he bought a brocade evening bag for Charity. There were bright threads of green in the pattern to match her eyes, and Adam smiled to think of her pleasure as he presented her with it. "You surely didn't think I'd be sour grapes," he'd say. . . . And if things were not going smoothly between Charity and Billy? . . . "A little remembrance to make you feel better, Chary." . . . While the woman was wrapping the bag, Adam's eyes fell on a small Tyrolean carved angel. In a burst of good feeling he made arrangements to have it sent to Mrs. Cadwallader in Paris. He enclosed a card: "I do not look back on our brief meeting with any bitterness. Best of luck in all things, Adam Blessing." Adam spent the rest of his afternoon back in his room, recording the big day in his Journal. It was odd that as much as he had looked forward to this time, now that it was here, he was not sure what he wanted to say about it. He described his purchases, made a note of his expenditures, and then wrote rather banal things like "What will we all say to one another?" and "Even the weather looks promising, seems to be cooling off."

At twenty minutes to six, Adam left the Delle Nazioni, packages under his arm, his heart pounding under his jacket. A peddler near the taxi-stand was selling some blue and yellow flowers. Adam decided that to-morrow he would drop a postcard to that florist on Madison and 96th. Say something short and nice, like: "Visiting here with Charity Cadwallader and Billy Bollin. Did you know they were married? Best wishes, Mr. Blessing." Before Adam got into the taxi, he paid for a bunch of the flowers, but refused to take them when the peddler held them out. "Give them to your wife!" Adam smiled. The peddler shook his head, not understanding. *"Moglie! Moglie!"* Adam said, pleased that he had remembered the Italian for "wife." The peddler nodded and said, *"Si, Moglie!"* trying to give the flowers to Adam again. Adam pointed at the peddler. *"Your moglie!"* . . . The peddler made a face at Adam. He looked angry, and as Adam got into the taxi, he believed the peddler was cursing him. Adam could not understand it, and as he rode to the Mediterraneo, his feelings were hurt; there was a slight edge off the evening; a blemish, ever so small.

"Addie?" a voice behind him said.

Adam whirled around in the Mediterraneo's lobby and shouted, "Billy! Billy! My God, Billy!"

"All right," Billy said. "Let's calm down, Addie."

Billy was not smiling, and slowly Adam's broad grin faded from his face.

Billy was saying that they could have a drink at the bar, and he was walking ahead, with Adam following, a bit dazed by Billy's abruptness. In appearance, Billy was the same; still dressed as neatly and elegantly as ever. His back was to Adam, but already Adam had begun to admire the silver-blue nubby-silk dinner jacket Billy was wearing, with the dark evening pants and black pumps. Billy pointed to a small table in a corner.

"Sit down," said Billy. "Scotch?"

Adam had intended to sip a sherry, go very easy, but he was so bewildered by Billy's cool greeting, he agreed to the whisky.

Billy spoke Italian to a waiter standing nearby, then he sat down at the table opposite Adam.

"It's good to see you," said Adam. "I'm sorry I'm not dressed."

Billy was looking him over carefully, wordlessly.

"What's the beard for, Addie?"

"It's not a disguise or anything," Adam forced a chuckle. "You know . . . in Europe and all."

"Taken on a little weight, haven't you, Addie?"

"It's this suit," said Adam. Billy made him nervous, staring hard at him that way. Adam added, "Oh, I suppose you mean my face is fuller. I guess it is."

"Everything is, Addie," said Billy.

"*You* look the same, Billy."

"I am the same."

"Well, good! I couldn't be more pleased!"

There were several moments of awkward silence then, broken by the waiter's arrival with Adam's Scotch. After the waiter left the table, Billy leaned forward, his elbows resting on the table top. "Now, let's get everything straight right now, Addie, all right?"

A chill ran through Adam. "Yes. How are you? How is everything going?"

"The first thing we'll get straight, Addie, is that how *I* am, and how things are going with *me,* is none of *your* goddam business!"

Adam gulped while he lived through another chill. Billy said, "I wrote you the week before I left Switzerland and told you to get out of my apartment. Let's start there. You stayed on until the end of August."

"I didn't take you seriously, was all, Billy. I get mad an say mean things, too . . . I just—didn't take you seriously."

"What did you take seriously, Addie?"

"Look, Billy, you never wrote after that, did you? Not a word! Not one word! I had to read about your marriage in the newspapers! How did you think I felt?"

"I didn't write after that because I thought you knew enough to get the hell out when someone tells you to!"

Adam took a gulp of his whisky. "You're not using a very nice tone of voice, Billy. We all make mistakes!"

"Mistakes!" Billy rolled his eyes back in his head and hit his palm with his fist. "You were harassing the Cadwalladers to a point where they were threatening to call the police! Do you think you were welcome in my place after that!"

Another gulp of whisky . . . Adam said, "Yesterday I had drinks with Mrs. Cadwallader—no it was the day before. Anyway, I'm telling you the truth. We had drinks and today I bought her a gift right here on the Via Frattina, Billy!"

"I know all about the day before yesterday, and if I were you, Addie, I'd cancel the gift."

"She told me you were in Rome. What would she have told me that for, if she didn't like me?"

"We all make mistakes, as you say, Addie. Mrs. Cadwallader called us to warn us you were around."

"I'll have another drink," Adam said, draining his glass.

"Not with me, mister!"

"What's the point in asking me for *one* drink?" Adam said.

"Addie, goddam it, *I* didn't ask you!"

"No," Adam said, "you didn't." His eyes were a blur of tears. He hoped Billy could not see them in the dim light. If he could change the subject, it would be O.K. . . . he could get hold . . . he had not really lost hold yet. "I like your dinner jacket very much," he said. "Did you have it made here?" He did not trust himself to raise his head and look into Billy's eyes, fearing tears would roll from his own. He said, "Since my money—since I came into it, I've not gone in for flashy things myself. I've always been more conservative."

"That's another thing," said Billy, "this money you've come into! Christ, Addie, why kid yourself! You must have about a thousand dollars of that money left!"

"The Mart was worth more than that, Billy. You never thought I could become involved in a big business, did you? Well, I was."

"I suppose you're going to tell me you sold out?" Billy was holding his glass, rubbing the sweat off the sides of it with his finger, eyeing Adam suspiciously.

"Yes, I sold out. What did you think?"

"I *know*," said Billy. "I don't have to think, Addie. I met an old friend of yours a month or so ago. Dorothy Schackleford, remember her, Addie?"

"She wasn't a particular friend. She doesn't know my business!"

"She was a better friend than you deserved, mister. She

told me the only thing you got from that whole deal was that album that belonged to Goethe's son, the one you showed off that night we all met for the first time." Billy sipped his Scotch, finishing it, signaling for the waiter as he said, "She told me you got about $50,000—period, which wasn't bad pickings for a clerk!"

Adam laughed. "I don't care if you do know I was a clerk! You think I care?"

"Enough to *lie!* What'd you lie for? Christ, Addie, you're such a goddam small-time snob!"

"Dorothy Schackleford doesn't know anything about me or my money!"

"Keep your voice down, Addie."

"Let people stare! Do you think I'm not used to it?"

"I just bet you're very used to it!"

"You're not my friend," Adam said, and now the tears were starting, down his cheeks. He took out his handkerchief and brushed them away. Billy watched him with a look of disgust. The waiter came, and Adam said, "Another for me!"

The waiter looked questioningly at Billy, but Billy shook his head. "I'm leaving," he said to Adam.

"I have something for you. For you and Charity." Adam took the packages from under the small table. "Look, I have something."

"We don't want your gifts, Addie. Thanks just the same."

"But I bought them for you! They're wedding presents."

"It's a little late for that, Addie."

"Why? Something's wrong, isn't it? Things aren't going well, are they?"

Billy stood up. He tossed some large paper bills on the table. "Dorothy Schackleford's working here in Rome, in case you're interested, Addie. You could probably benefit by looking her up. She works for the Fellow's Rome Foundation. Some kind of *missionary* work . . . Good-by, Addie." He started out the door, but Adam jumped up and ran after him. "Your presents!" he said; "if you don't want yours, at least take Charity's!"

"She doesn't want hers either, Addie!"

Billy had stopped, just outside the entranceway of the

bar. He was fairly gritting his teeth, his eyes narrowed, his words very nearly forced out of the sides of his mouth, softly, slowly: "You've turned into some kind of nut, mister! I don't know what kind and I don't give a goddam, but stay out of my way, I warn you!"

"Hit me," Adam said, "go ahead and hit me, if you want to!"

"Beggar!" Billy said, "You beggar!" And he left Adam standing there, holding the gifts, trembling. . . .

14

Safety Deposit-South Orange, N.J.	
(Savings and Trust)	*$10,000*
In $20 bills, black suitcase, (802)	*$16,040*
In $50 bills, cowhide suitcase (400)	*$20,000*
In Traveller's Checks (Am. Express)	*$10,000*
Spent since September:	*$19,560*
	$75,600

FROM ADAM BLESSING'S JOURNAL

"You have been so very kind," said Adam to his new friend.

"Nonsense," Ernesto Leogrande said. "I am bored with the way my people treat the American tourists."

Adam had been quite drunk when Leogrande had come up to him in the bar opposite the Mediterraneo. Leogrande had prevented the waiter from overcharging Adam by a thousand lire, after which he helped Adam leave, supporting Adam by crossing one of Adam's arms over his shoulder. At another bar, he had gotten a coffee for Adam, and sat with him while Adam sipped it slowly and pulled himself together. He had brought Adam to this small *trattoria* on the Portico di Ottavia.

Adam said, "It's not the money, Ernesto. I hope you believe that. I was just treated rather cruelly by a life-long friend, then for a perfect stranger to help me—well, I appreciate it."

"Sì,sì—" Leogrande brushed aside Adam's gratitude, and took another stab at his veal. He was a large, hook-nosed Italian with a sunburned face and straight, dark eyebrows, black wavy hair and a wide white smile. He wore a light blue shirt open at the neck, a brown-and-black checkered sport coat, and light blue slacks. While he ate and drank, he smoked a cigarette that rested in the plastic ashtray beside his plate, and around his neck on a silver chain he wore a religious medal. His English was good. He was from Civitavecchia, he told Adam. His family ran a *pensione* there, and all spoke English. He was in Rome on a holiday.

Adam said, "I insist on taking you to dinner, Ernesto."

"No, no, forget that! You are my guest. Besides, hang on to your money. Rome is expensive. Save enough to come to Civitavecchia. We have a good beach. You like to swim?"

"I never learned," Adam said. "I was fat as a boy. I was afraid I would sink."

Ernesto threw his head back and laughed as though Adam was a great comedian, and Adam joined in, warmed by his friend's congeniality.

"Don't worry about my money," said Adam. "I have enough."

"But be careful in Rome, Adam. All the hands are open."

"I insist on taking you to dinner," Adam said again. "Really, Ernesto, I have enough money and more!"

Leogrande changed the subject. He told Adam that this section where they were dining was the old Ghetto.

"Some say the persecution of the Jews was bad with Hitler," said Ernesto, "but here in the Middle Ages, much worse." He told Adam that it used to be during Carnivale that the Romans rounded up the Jews and made them run races down the whole length of the Corso, naked. "Cruelty," he said, "such terrible cruelty! What's the matter with mankind anyway, Adam?"

Adam had never talked very confidentially with anyone but Mrs. Auerbach. He found himself able to open up with Ernesto, and he told him quite a lot about Billy and Charity. "You mentioned cruelty awhile ago," he told him. "How do you think I felt when after all this time I was brushed off like a fly by Billy? I didn't even see Chary. I call her that. Pet name."

"A sad tale," said Ernesto. "Tonight we eat and drink and forget, Adam! How about that?"

The idea appealed to Adam immensely. He would be all right with Ernesto, no matter how much he drank. The trouble in the past was that he had been alone, with no one to talk to. He felt as though he could tell Ernesto anything, almost anything. The pair ordered another litre of Frascati, and clinked their glasses together in a toast to the Alban Hills, where the wine came from, Ernesto said. Ernesto was a great talker. The *trattoria* was within sight of the theater of Marcellus, and looming over the whole area was the huge, gloomy Palazzo Cenci. Ernesto told Adam about the Cenci family and the hideous crimes that stained the family name. Adam listened while he imagined himself dining at this spot with Billy and Charity, expounding as Ernesto did on the history of the area, ordering more Frascati, proposing the toast to the Alban Hills—all of it, while Billy and Charity admired his intimacy with this unfamiliar part of Rome, complimented him, perhaps, on his remarkable acclimation to Europe.

". . . and I mean every crime imaginable," Ernesto was saying, "that was the Cenci family for you. Rape, murder, incest, torture—and plain old-fashioned robbery! No excuse for it—man's inhumanity to man!" He poured more wine in both their glasses. "But I do all the talking, Adam. You talk."

"What did you think of the Zumbach kidnapping?" said Adam.

"Detestable!"

"Yes. I thought so, too. At least the other one—the one in our country was not so bad."

Ernesto said. "I remember hearing of your Lindbergh child."

"Oh, this Schneider case was different. The child was returned safely."

"And his kidnappers?"

"There was only one, I think."

"Usually there are two, no?"

"I think only one in the Schneider case. A civilized sort, you know what I mean, Ernesto? He never harmed a hair on the child's head."

"Ah, well . . . crime is crime." Ernesto picked up the check and began adding it up.

"Please," said Adam, "I would like to pay for this. I have plenty of money on me."

Ernesto, with a wave of his hand, brushed aside Adam's offer. "On me," he said, "and in Civitavecchia, you stay at our place."

"I'll pay," said Adam.

Ernesto smiled. "Of course . . . there, I am in business."

"I'll come as soon as I can," said Adam. "I may even bring friends with me, my friends I told you about."

"You have forgiven them already?"

"Well——" Adam hesitated. Ernesto leaned across the table and gave Adam a friendly push with his long arm. He said, "Ah, you, you are a softie! I like you, my friend. I consider you my friend."

Adam's whole being was swollen with sudden joy.

After Ernesto paid the bill, the pair decided to have still another drink. Strega, Ernesto suggested, just the thing. Adam was a little drunk, but it was a pleasant sort of intoxication, warm and easy, not sloppy, and the only urgency, Adam's growing desire to tell Ernesto more about himself. They had a Strega after the first, and one after the second, and Adam told Ernesto how Mrs. Auerbach had left him everything, and how her sister had come along and taken it all away from him.

"But how do you have anything?" Ernesto said.

"She left me one piece of stock worth plenty of money," said Adam, and he felt bad that he had lied to his friend at their very first meeting. He wanted to undo the lie and tell Ernesto the truth, and he was very nearly on the verge of doing just that, when suddenly Ernesto said, "Well, how about it, Adam, we find some girls now!"

"Girls?" Adam blinked, dumfounded. He had expected to stay on drinking with Ernesto, the two of them together in a great camaraderie.

"Girls!" Ernesto said again, "we're forgetting everything tonight, aren't we?"

"I thought we would be by ourselves," Adam said, "talk more, and have more Strega."

"Three is all the Stregas we need. Too sweet. There's wine where the girls are, Adam! C'mon!" He was getting up, shoving his chair back, taking a long toothpick from his jacket and digging at his mouth with it. "It's not far away either. We can walk."

"Are you sure we want to?" Adam said. He remained sitting at the table.

Ernesto looked down at him, taking the toothpick from his mouth a moment, his face thoughtful. "Hey, there's not anything wrong with you, is there?"

"What do you mean?"

"You like girls, Adam, don't you?"

Adam's face felt hot, and he became angry. "Of course! What do you think I've been telling you about my Chary! What's the matter with you anyway! I've been following her all over Europe!" Adam was disappointed in Ernesto for having such a thought. He had imagined Ernesto knew him like a brother, instantly.

Ernesto laughed, came around and clapped Adam on the back. "All right then! Let's go! It's the only way to forget your Chary, my friend. I know a girl who can make a man forget his last name!"

Adam got up. He said, "But I may be too drunk."

"This girl," Ernesto laughed, "can take care of that too!"

To get there, Adam and Ernesto had to make their way through twisting streets, where the houses huddled together, their shutters closed against the heat, giving the appearance that no one lived in them; there were no lights, and only vague signs of life—a cat prowling in an ashcan, an old man on a front stoop asleep with his head in his arms, a couple pressed against the side of a building making love, and in an alleyway a few doors from their destination, a drunk urinating.

Adam smiled back at Ernesto uncertainly, and then he found himself standing in a kitchen of an old house with his friend. In the sink as they entered, a candle stuck into a wine bottle, was the only light. Ernesto called: *"Signora! Subito! Ai! Signora!"*

A thin old woman came rushing out, shushing him. She wore a bright green satin dress, and a matching ribbon in her gray hair, rouge and eye make-up, shiny black high-heels, with no stockings and ugly blue veins on pale white legs. Ernesto spoke to her in rapid Italïan, only some of which Adam caught. An American, Ernesto said, a nice girl for him, young but not too young, and other things Adam could not understand. Then there was some dickering about money, ending with Ernesto's emphatic: "Ten thousand lire!" The thin woman frowned and Ernesto pinched her cheeks, which made her laugh and agree.

"They don't know any English," said Ernesto to his companion, "so you are in a sinking ship together, ah?" He laughed, and punched Adam's arm playfully. "But before the ship goes down, you—" he made an obscene gesture. Then he left through the beaded curtains with a blond girl, who appeared suddenly and the thin woman pushed a brunette in Adam's direction. She was smoking a cigarette, the hot ash dangerously close to her lips, her hands folded across an immense bosom. She shrugged and walked toward Adam, indicating with her thumb that he should follow her. He held out the lire to her, and with another jerk of her thumb, she indicated that he should give it to the thin woman. Then Adam followed her down a dark and narrow hall, into a very small room, with a bed in it, a screen hiding what seemed to be another sink, a white bowl on a table beside the bed, and a hassock with fringes on its side. The girl took her clothes off without a word. Adam removed his shirt, and stood helplessly by the bed. The naked girl came across the carpet scratching her arms, lighting another cigarette. Adam sat on the bed and removed his shoes. From behind the bed table, the girl took out a bottle of wine. She offered some to Adam in a dirty glass. He wanted to decline, but he wanted a drink just as badly.

She spoke to him in Italian. "Is that all?" meaning, was that all he was going to take off.

Adam shrugged, and she shrugged. She said, "Ready?"

Adam sighed. He started to undo his pants. The girl

walked over and began to help him. "You don't want to take them off?"

"No."

She bent and tried to kiss him. She smelled of something like rotten peach pits, and Adam could not bear it. He turned away. The girl asked him a question he could not understand. She repeated it, and he understood the sentence after: "Is that what you want?"

"Drunk," said Adam, and in Italian: "Intoxicated."

In English the girl said, "I take care. I know."

She pushed Adam back in a gentle way which surprised him, and he realized as his head hit the pillow and he shut his eyes, that he was dizzy, that his drinks had caught up with him at last. It did not matter at all, for he found out that nothing was expected of him, and afterwards, he slept.

15

Dear Billy and Chary,

How is everything? I hope you are enjoying your stay in Roma as I am. After I left Billy last night at the Mediterraneo, I went across the street and had some drinks. I made the acquaintance of a very nice chap from Civitavecchia—a real Italian! We went on the town together, and believe me, it was great fun! We hope to do it again very soon.

I left your wedding presents with the desk clerk. You don't have to thank me. I realize they are long overdue, but then we sort of lost track of one another, didn't we? Bygones be bygones—here we are in The Eternal City! How about having dinner with me one night this week? There's a fascinating *trattoría* on Portico di Ottavia, where I would like you to be my guests. Please call me here at the hotel any day between noon and two. I'll wait for your call.

Believe me I hope your marriage is a great success!

Billy mentioned Dorothy Schackleford the other

night, saying she had a job here. I would like her address, if it is not any trouble. How on earth did you get together with her, not that I have anything against her —just curious.

If I seemed slightly nervous the other night, please understand that I was under some strain. I have been traveling incessantly this past year. I kept thinking I'd run into you, but no such luck. Anyway, as I said, here we are reunited. Let's make the most of it. I'll be waiting to hear from you.

Always,
Adam.

Adam had written the note to Billy and Charity three days ago, the morning he returned from his night with Ernesto. Before he had parted from his new friend, he had loaned him a little less than twenty-five dollars. Ernesto explained that the blond had helped herself to his wallet, that after he got some sleep he would go back to the house and demand the return of his money.

"You have to watch their kind," said Ernesto, "and to think they would try it with me, a good customer!"

"I have a funny feeling, Ernesto, that I talked to the girl I was with, told her some things I don't want anyone to know."

Ernesto had laughed, "She speaks no English, Adam! Forget it!"

"It may have been a dream anyway."

"A dream, of course. You were fast asleep when I pounded on your door. She must have been good."

The conversation had taken place at dawn on the Via Monte Cenci. They shook hands, Ernesto explaining that he stayed within walking distance, that Adam would find a taxi-stand three blocks over. Ernesto said he would come to Adam's hotel the next night, when he got his money back. He would repay Adam then.

"I wish you would just keep it, Ernesto, a gift from me."

"Nah! Nah!" And with a wave of his hand, "Tomorrow, Adam," he was gone.

Now he sat opposite Adam, in Adam's small room at the Delle Nazioni. He smoked a cigar and wore the same brown-and-black checkered sport coat, and blue slacks. His shirt was different, a gaudy yellow one with Aloha written across it countless times in blue, and white flowers splashed in between. Adam would have liked to give him one of his shirts, but he was familiar with Ernesto's stubborn pride.

"So you thought I would not show up, ah?" Ernesto laughed.

"I'm glad you're here. Not for the money." When Ernesto had entered the room, the first thing he had done was to slap the fifteen thousand lire onto the bureau top.

"What have you done since Wednesday, Adam?"

"Nothing, really."

"You have no business?"

"Oh, I have investments, you see, Ernesto."

"Good! I like to have my friends free from care!" Ernesto walked around Adam's room puffing on his cigar, admiring a tie of Adam's ("You can have it", said Adam —Ernesto would not hear of it) and Adam's military brushes, and his cowhide luggage. Adam watched him, wishing he could have the courage to unburden himself to Ernesto. Adam could still not get it out of his mind that he had told the brunette—everything. Still it was all mixed up with a dream of meeting the Cenci family, and running naked down the length of the Corso, while Billy laughed and threw poodle-shaped cuff links with ruby eyes, at his body.

Over a bottle of Maccarese Adam sent for, they talked. Ernesto told Adam of his father's illness, which he had heard of just two days ago. "Serious," said Ernesto, "and perhaps it will mean I will take a job for a while here in Rome." He explained that his sisters could help his mother run their place in Civitavecchia; that it would be better if he found something to pay well. Guide work, he thought; he had once worked as a guide at the Colosseum, another time as one in the Palazzo Pitti in Florence.

"But Ernesto," Adam interrupted, "let me help you. Let me lend you money for your father."

Ernesto looked embarrassed. He changed the subject immediately. Did Adam like the brunette the other night?

"I'm sorry," he said, not waiting for Adam's answer; "she was probably a pig. I hear she takes everything off. Even among whores that is thought indecent. A good whore, Adam, always keeps her stockings on. There is an expression we have here. We say that a whore who takes her stockings off is not in business. You see? She enjoys taking her clothes off. A whore is not supposed to enjoy her work. Only a pig-whore." He bit the end off another cigar, which he took from his shirt pocket. "The occupation spoiled her, Adam. She knew all the soldiers, always joking and laughing with the Germans. Then with the Americans."

Adam's heart missed a beat. "But she doesn't know English?"

"Who knows what a pig knows, Adam?"

"But you said she didn't."

"She probably doesn't."

"Ernesto," said Adam, "The other night she said something in English to me. I remember. She said it very plainly: 'I'll take care of you.' I believe that was it."

Ernesto grunted: "You should have shoved her face in the wall, the pig. I hope you told her you would take care of things, not her! They do anything to save their backs, their kind."

Adam was perspiring, his heart hammering. "You don't understand, Ernesto. I think I told her something. I don't know if I dreamed it, or if I told her—but she could get me in trouble, Ernesto, if I did say it—if she speaks English!"

"You, Adam? You're making a joke on me. What could you have done so bad! Forget it!"

"Ernesto, I'm telling you, it could get me in trouble."

Ernesto took his cigar out of his mouth, leaned forward in the leather chair and said, "My friend, you are serious, aren't you?"

"Yes. It's—well, a long story. It's—but I don't like to tell it." Adam was thinking that it was not that he did not trust Ernesto; it was that he was afraid Ernesto would dislike him. "Crime is crime," Ernesto had said the other night.

Ernesto stopped Adam from continuing. "You are in trouble?"

"Not yet. It's not really bad." He was remembering
that the other night when he told Ernesto how the Schneider boy had been returned without a scratch, Ernesto
seemed unsympathetic. Crime is crime . . . Adam said,
"It just might look bad. I wouldn't want someone like
that girl to know it."

"Are you sure she does?"

"No, no! That's just it. I'm in the dark! Ernesto, I'll
tell you about it. You see—"

But Ernesto held his large hand up. "Stop, Adam! Don't
trust anyone! I don't want to know, do you see? If you
are guilty of something, I don't want to know. Then you
would never think I gave you away."

"I'd never think that," said Adam.

"Good! But don't tell me. Trust no one, Adam, particularly not someone you know less than a week."

Adam smiled. "You are wonderful, Ernesto."

"Nah! Listen, my friend, I'll go and visit that place tonight. I'll find out if you said anything or not. Believe me,
I'll not listen to whatever it is, if you did say it. I'll stop
her from repeating it, but I'll find out. . . . If you said
something, well—that can be fixed. A pair of stockings,
a pretty dress—those pigs don't know enough to be vi-
cious. Besides, you probably exaggerate your wrong. I
know you."

Adam said, "I don't exaggerate it. . . . I could tell you
this much—"

"*Basta!*" Ernesto stopped him. "I don't want to hear."

They finished the bottle of Maccarese. Ernesto said he
must hunt a job. Adam was able to convince him to bor-
row at least a hundred dollars, half to buy clothes he
would need for a job (he had brought only a few shirts
for his holiday in Rome) and half to send immediately to
his father.

Adam planned to spend the afternoon searching for
another gift for Luther Schneider. He changed his
clothes and took a shower, then headed for the Via dei
Coronari, where there were antique shops specializing in
silver. At the Via Veneto, he could not resist stopping
for a cold beer. Over the drink he lost interest in his
afternoon's plan. Why should he buy Schneider any more

gifts? Schneider had really not had faith in him; he had simply feared for Timmy's life. The money Schneider had paid Adam was nothing to a man that rich, no more than the sixty thousand lire Adam had handed to Ernesto. Why had Adam not seen that before? It would be ridiculous to buy another gift for Schneider. Adam chuckled to himself. Ernesto had been right last night when he had called Adam a softie. Look at the way Billy and Chary were treating him, and after Adam had taken such pains to pick out presents they would enjoy. Adam wished he had told Ernesto about that! Ernesto would have had something to say about that sort of shabby treatment. Adam smiled as he finished his beer. He could see Ernesto's dark eyes flashing with anger, see him grabbing Billy by the fancy narrow shawl lapels of his dinner jacket, hear Ernesto shouting, "Adam is my friend, do you understand! Apologize to my friend!" . . . Adam ordered a Martini when he finished his beer. "What do you mean making a friend of mine wait around day after day for your phone call!" Ernesto would demand . . . "and don't call him Addie any more!" said Ernesto over Adam's third Martini, and gently, Adam put his hand on Ernesto's arm to restrain him. A look of gratitude came in Billy's eyes. "Thank you, Adam. Thanks a lot." . . .

It was anger that made Billy's eyes so hard.

"How the hell much longer are you going to keep this up!"

Instinct, impulse—whatever it was that had led Adam toward the vicinity of the Via Nazionale, onto the Via Cavour, to the Mediterraneo, it was opportunely timed. Adam stepped over Billy's luggage, walking right past Billy as he stood holding open the door to his room. "Where are you going?" Adam said. "Were you going without telling me, Billy?"

"You know, Addie, you're sick! I mean, you're very sick!" Billy let the door swing shut, and he crossed to one of the twin beds and an open suitcase into which he was putting shirts and balls of socks. "Why don't you go see a doctor, Addie?"

"You're not wearing your present," Adam said. Billy was wearing a green robe with a faint charcoal gray stripe in it, some sort of cotton fabric, with a shirt under it, and light gray pants.

"Okay, Addie, let's stop talking about the presents. They're right where you left them, at the downstairs desk. I'd pick them up on my way out, if I were you, exchange them. And incidentally, Addie," he said, turning and facing Adam with the same hard look to his eyes, "When I was in New York this spring, I found out you were going around saying you were me. I got my cuff links back too. What's with you, Addie? Do you need a head-shrinker or something?"

Adam said, "Why do you live in the past so, Billy? Here we are in Rome together. Can't we be friendly?"

"You've been drinking, too," said Billy. "You never could drink, could you?" He slipped his robe off then, and began folding it. "Why don't you lay off the stuff? See your friend Dorothy Schackleford. I tell you she's with some group who helps people."

"Ever since we were children you've wanted to insult me and hurt my feelings, haven't you, Billy?"

"Rubbish!" Billy dropped the folded robe on the shirts in his suitcase. "Here, I'll write down her address. I've got it somewhere here in my book." He was fumbling through the pages of a small, green leather address book, with fleurs-de-lys stamped on it. From Florence, Adam thought; Adam had bought a cigarette case, the stamping identical . . . so they had been to Florence, too, and he had missed them there as well. Or had they been running from him? Were they running from him now, again? And where was Chary? Why hadn't he seen Chary yet?

"Here it is," said Billy. "I'll jot it down for you. . . . You know, Adam, you have a tendency to exaggerate almost everything. For example this crap about our being childhood friends. Now you know damn well who I hung around with—Dick Nolan and Pete MacGuire . . . Now hell, Addie, why aren't you just more realistic? We only saw each other two or three times a month when we were kids! Here—" he handed Adam a card with an address scribbled on it. "We ran into Dorothy one afternoon on the Via Veneto. She asked about you."

Billy closed the lid of the suitcase, and snapped the

silver locks. "That does it," he said. "Well, Addie—" holding out his hand, "This is it."

"And Chary? Where's Chary?"

"She's not here, obviously!"

"Then there is trouble!" Adam smiled. He sat down on the bed. "I knew it wouldn't be long before it all came out."

"There isn't any trouble Addie, and you have to get out now."

"Without seeing Chary?" Adam's eyes began to fill.

"And cut out the Chary, Addie! Since when do *you* call her Chary!"

"It's too bad you're leaving before you meet my new business partner," said Adam. "His name is Ernesto. We're opening a beach club in Civitavecchia." As he said it, Adam decided it was a very good idea. He and Ernesto could expand his family's *pensione*.

Billy was running around checking drawers and closets for anything he might have forgotten. Adam said, "We're opening a very interesting club, the club—" he searched for some name, thought of Ernesto's shirt with Aloha splashed across it, and after a few more bullet associations, said: "The State Fifty, is what we're calling it. We're sort of using a Hawaiian theme. We might even call it The Fiftieth Star. We don't have it all figured out yet," said Adam, following Billy around back and forth as he talked. "We have long discussions about it. What do *you* think we ought to call it, Billy?"

Billy slammed the door of the bathroom cabinet, colliding with Adam in the entranceway. "Get the hell out of here, will you, Addie, or do I have to call the manager!"

Adam was stunned. He had felt that everything had been going all right, and now Billy had suddenly turned on him, without any explanation.

"Billy," said Adam, "it's a wonder you have any friends."

Billy looked as though he were actually going to punch Adam in the nose then, but as he took a step forward, a key turned in the lock, and into the room came Charity.

"Chary!" Adam said. There was a small spray of babies'-breath pinned to her light gray suit, and her black hair was piled on top of her head, and held by silver combs; and at her ears, silver loop earrings, like gypsys', but she was not smiling, merely looking at Adam as though he were a bellhop or some other casual intruder. And again, Adam exclaimed, "Chary!" and began walking toward her.

All at once, she began to giggle, and the giggle grew into laughter, and Adam stood before her bewildered as she tossed her head back the way a man might, and laughed that very hard, wild, uncontrollable way there is of laughing.

"Oh my, migod," she managed, before another fit of the same type laughter, while Adam stood very embarrassed, yet distracted from his embarrassment slightly by the thought that something was different about Chary.

"You've changed," he said.

"*I* have, oh, Addie, my, migod!" and there seemed to be no end to her laughter.

Billy, who had come around to stand beside her, was even smiling, and for the barest few seconds Adam thought that here it was as he had always planned it, the three of them together, joking, old friends, and Adam grinned broadly, stroked his beard, his eyes twinkling at his friends. Ah, this is the way it should always have been, and would have been too had I ever caught up with you last fall . . . he said to them, "You know I've looked forward to this moment for eons!" And it dawned on him then why Chary looked different. She too had taken on some weight.

"Your added weight becomes you," said Adam.

She had turned to Billy and was telling him something about train times. Adam tried to hear, but she spoke too low.

"But wait a minute," Adam said, "We're not going to leave it at this, are we? Aren't we at least all going to have dinner tonight?"

"Out!" Billy said suddenly. He was pointing at the door with his finger, watching Adam carefully, waiting for Adam to go, of all things.

It must be a joke, and Adam laughed. "Down, boy!" he said, making his own joke. He smiled at Chary. "You really look good with that added weight. You ought to stay that way."

She put her hand to her mouth, palm in, as though she were going to catch something—a pit of some sort, or as though she might cough or sneeze, and Adam was slightly surprised to see she was simply laughing again—trying hard not to, but there you are—it was laughter, choked back. He wondered if she were herself.

"Why is Chary so silly? Is she doped up or something?"

Adam thought of the way Timmy used to giggle just as the sleeping pills took; the way Timmy would chuckle in his sleep.

"Come on, Addie!" and now Billy was actually pulling Adam along by the arm.

"Make him stop, Char!" Adam said.

"That's right, Adam. Ask a pregnant woman for help!" said Billy.

Pregnant. Chary was pregnant—that was the difference.

"It's still not too late, Chary," Adam said. "If you're not happy, it's my fault, and I'll still—" but he could not finish. He felt dizzy suddenly, very strange, and tired too. Gin always made him tired. "Let go, let go," his own voice sounded far away to him, but Billy took his hands off Adam. He said, "Go on now, Addie. We try to be nice, but it's way out of hand now."

"Yes," Adam said. "It is."

He remembered something Melnik had said to him. "You didn't get yourself into this mess because of that girl. You hardly know that girl. You can't fight an enemy by boxing with the shadow."

Billy was facing him then, and Adam staggered a bit as he moved toward him. He caught hold of Billy's shoulders, and it was in his mind to strike Billy, but instead, he began to try to tickle him.

"What the hell!" Billy shoved him away.

"I only wanted you to laugh," said Adam. He could see Charity's face over Billy's shoulder. The expression was grave now, she was frowning, and her eyes squinting, as though she must look very hard to believe what she saw.

Adam said, "Yes, it's me, Chary. It's Adam."

"Billy, let's get some help," she said.

They were both regarding him in a most peculiar way,

as though there were actually something very wrong with him.

Adam held his forehead with his hand. "I—have to use your bathroom," he said.

"The hell—" Billy started to say, but it was too late already. Suddenly before he could reach anywhere, Adam was ill. Over the noise of his own vomiting, he could hear Billy cursing, violently, obscenely. Chary had run to the telephone. Adam began to cry and vomit at the same time. Billy only cared about his suitcases, and he was busy pulling them out of the way, but they were already soiled.

16

> *"From Venice, a postcard saying Chary had a boy, 6 lbs. There is no reason to suspect they would name it after me, and I did not even broach the possibility to Dorothy, but it does not seem unlikely."*

FROM ADAM BLESSING'S JOURNAL

Adam glanced at his watch. She was already ten minutes late. Later and later getting off to her meetings every time Ernesto came by. It had been going on for a month. He had moved into Dorothy's small apartment on the Via Po, the day after Billy and Chary left Rome. Since then he had not touched liquor, not even so much as a glass of wine with his meals; and as he had promised Dorothy, he had not tried to communicate with Billy and Chary, though he knew the address of their apartment in Venice. Occasionally they sent Dorothy a card, and Adam thought how like Billy that was, to pretend a friendship with her, while he ignored Adam. Billy only did it to spite Adam, of that Adam was convinced, but he let Dorothy think what she wanted to.

"You should be glad they called me instead of the police," Dorothy had said to him once.

"But I have no reason to fear the police," Adam told her.

"You just don't get the point, Adam"—her answer.

It was Dorothy Schackleford who did not get the point. She believed everything Billy said, all about Adam making Chary afraid that night he had gone to their room at the Mediterraneo, all about Adam acting "strangely," every lie Billy told. Now she wanted to help Adam. Adam, she said, was an alcoholic. She had even tried to drag him to one of her "meetings." "You can't just wander around all day with nothing to do," she said; "once you admit you're an alcoholic, you're free, Adam. You can look for work, do something with your life" . . . Adam smiled to himself. He had plans. He let her go on thinking that he had inherited the *Stammbuch* from Mrs. Auerbach, that he was living off *that* money. He even tolerated her harangues about his lack of feeling. Adam did not feel anything, she said, not for anyone. What was the matter with Adam anyway? . . . He supposed she had still never gotten over being stood up by Adam on the evening of Mrs. Auerbach's service. Sometimes when she accused Adam of not even being grateful to Mrs. Auerbach for leaving him the *Stammbuch,* he felt like shouting out the truth. Instead, he sat listening to her with a small grin tipping his lips. He could take it. He knew the score. He could see that before very long, Dorothy Schackleford would turn against him too. Women had always let Adam down in a way that made him look as though he had done the wrong. More and more lately, he thought of the faceless woman plopped down on the straight-back wooden chair in the kitchen of years-ago: "And a lot *you* care!" she had said. . . . "And a lot *you* care!"

Dorothy Schackleford finally left for her meeting, not without admonishing Adam for the hundredth time, "Not even a beer now, Adam. Nothing!"

"She really has love for you, Adam," said Ernesto.

"She wants to save me," Adam said. They chuckled and Ernesto said, "Still—it is nice someone cares, ah?"

"*If* someone does," said Adam. "People have been known to marry people without caring for them, even have babies with them."

"That again!" Ernesto grunted. "Hey, let's go to the park! I have new things to work out with you, Adam."

"I wish we would do more than talk," Adam told him. "Isn't our place built yet?"

"Adam, it is not America. You wait until you see poor little Civitavecchia. Labor is cheap, but not plentiful."

"I want to see it," said Adam. "Why can't we go there and see it?"

Ernesto said, "In time. It will be a big surprise all at once. Then we'll tell Dorothy all about it, too."

Sometimes when Adam was alone during the daytime, when he took long walks through the Borghese Gardens, he fantasized that one day far-off, Luther Schneider would visit Civitavecchia, even bring Timmy with him. Adam would see that they got the best of everything. He would stop by their table and chat with them. In some of Adam's fantasies, he would hand Schneider an envelope which contained every single cent he owed him, with interest besides. In others, he would hand Schneider a card which said: ADAMO'S, Civitavecchia, Italy—Manager: Adam Blessing. Owner: Luther Schneider.

Schneider would say: "You know, son, originally I expressed faith in you simply because I feared for Timmy's safety. But now . . . Adam, I think of you the same way I think of Timmy."

They would become devoted to one another, Schneider and Adam.

Schneider would say: "I love Timmy, but he's never been a real son to me, poor little devil. *You* though, Adam—"

Strolling by the ilex trees in the Villa Borghese that evening, Ernesto seemed worried.

"Is something going wrong, Ernesto?"

"You are perceptive, Adam, one of the most perceptive people I have ever known. It was not my intention to burden you with more troubles."

"But, I haven't had to do any of the worrying, Ernesto. You've done everything!"

It was true. Ernesto had handled everything. From the very beginning, when Adam had proposed the club in Civitavecchia, it was Ernesto who had gotten an architect to draw up the plans, hassled with builders for a moderate price, gone back and forth to Civitavecchia to pick the land, and oversee the installation of the groundwork; and it was Ernesto who had handled the whole emergency with the equipment, when the workers were drilling for water. Had it not been for his friend, that emergency would have cost Adam ten times the amount. Ernesto's fiery ways, and his familiarity with the region and its people, had been a priceless asset. Ernesto had refused Adam's offer of a regular salary. He had been hurt by it. Since his father had recovered so rapidly from his illness, there was no more emergency, Ernesto pointed out, and he would live on his savings until the club was operating. Adam was accustomed to Ernesto's proud ways by now. As eager as he was to go to Civitavecchia with Ernesto and see the progress that had been made already, he understood Ernesto's reluctance to have Adam see anything before it was perfect. In the past two weeks, he had snapped a few pictures of the place under construction, but even these he was apologetic about. "You really can't tell how it will be," he would say. "I hate to even show you them, but I know your eagerness." Adam felt a thrill of accomplishment when he viewed the photographs. At last he was on his way to what Melnik had prescribed: a business of his own, and it would be a busy one at that.

"Adam, I worry. We are spending too much of your money."

"But that isn't so!"

"I feel bad about letting that rotten whore bribe you!"

"Forget that, Ernesto. A thousand dollars—that was cheap! Listen, I could have been taken for much more. Why won't you let me tell you about it?"

Ernesto shook his head. "No. I don't want to hear. I never should have taken you there in the first place. I feel bad about it."

"We have so much to look forward to," said Adam.

"I've forgotten all about that whore. Besides, I may not even have told her anything!"

"All the worse. I paid her your money for nothing then."

Adam said, "Ernesto, I don't care! I've forgotten it!"

"Now in Civitavecchia, more bad news."

"Your father?"

Ernesto sighed and shook his head. "No, Adam. It's the installation of the air-conditioning. The way it is now, the lines can't hold that much power. If we are going to have air-conditioning throughout Adamo's, we have to make arrangements for extra lines, to connect farther down. Otherwise we knock out everyone's electricity in the area."

"Is that all?" Adam laughed, and clapped his arm around his friend's shoulder. "I thought your father was taking a turn for the worse."

"I am a thrifty man, Adam."

"I know, but we have to put more money into it, that's all."

"I worry that we will run out."

"Dorothy's been talking to you," said Adam. "Isn't that true?"

He knew that whenever Dorothy could, behind his back, she discussed Adam with Ernesto. It had been Ernesto's idea to tell her that he was in Rome buying equipment for a new place on the coast—his folks' place. Dorothy was always comparing Adam with Ernesto; look how busy *he* is, Adam; and aren't you ashamed sometimes when Ernesto comes to visit and you see how hard *he's* worked all week? . . . Again, Adam would sit listening with the grin tipping his lips . . . he would hear Dorothy off in the other room of her apartment, whispering to Ernesto about Adam's need to be busy, about Adam's money becoming depleted day by day. . . . Several times it had become nearly unbearable, and he had begged Ernesto to let him tell Dorothy, but always Ernesto wanted things to be perfect.

"She tells me you imagine things, Adam. Oh, I know women, but I don't want you to pretend with me that you have more than you do."

"I can prove it," said Adam, "Let me prove it."

"No, no, I don't want any proof! I trust you. We're partners."

"Then what are you worried about?"

"I'm afraid you will be shocked by the amount we need next, Adam. I wonder if you realize how expensive these things are. Me, I'm experienced, even with a place as small as my family's—but you, Adam."

"Well?" said Adam. "How much?"

"Another $25,000," Ernesto answered.

Adam laughed. "So! I'll make a trip to New York! That amount I don't have with me, but I can fly to New York and back in less than a week. To tell you the truth, I wouldn't mind a trip. I think—"

"I could probably get the figure down," Ernesto said. "Say, $15,000."

"Oh yes, I have that left. Yes."

Ernesto slapped Adam's knee. "Good! Then you don't have to leave. I'll get him down, Adam. I can. I can make different arrangements."

"I don't mind a trip. Really, Ernesto!" The more Adam thought about a quick trip to New York, the more the idea appealed to him.

"No!" Ernesto said flatly.

"Why?"

"Because I need your advice, my friend. This is a crucial time. We are nearing completion."

"But it would only take me—"

"No, Adam!"

Adam was surprised at the sharp tone. He turned and looked at his friend's face. . . . But Ernesto smiled then, the large white smile which always reassured Adam: "Adam," said Ernesto, "I have a fear of planes and of friends on them. Now you will not have to fly in an airplane, and I am glad!"

The next day at breakfast, Adam read in a guidebook of a shop named Sirotta on Via Sistina. Among the various items the shop specialized in, the words "babies' bibs" had caught Adam's eye.

17

Vittorio Gelsi, 42, of 7 Via Monte Cenci was arrested this morning after a murder attempt. His wife, Maria, is in the hospital. Her condition is reported as critical. During an argument over money, Gelsi admitted stabbing her in the back. Tonia Gelsi, his sister, called police. A sometime "guide" for various tourist agencies, Gelsi was once fired by The Italian-Rome Scenic Tours Association for accepting money in advance from tourists for reservations in non-existent beach hotels in Ostia, Civitavecchia and Umbria. He served a three-year sentence for this offence, and several other, smaller terms for pickpocketing and soliciting as a pimp.

FROM THE ROME AMERICAN

The *carabiniere* smiled at Adam. "But he has admitted it, *Signore*."

In Adam's hand were the photographs of Ernesto, the same he had seen in the newspaper, above the story of the murder attempt. Vittorio Gelsi, and after his name, a number.

The *carabiniere* said, "He has not take your money, I hope. He has take money from Americans before this thing."

"No," Adam lied.

"Why he call himself Ernesto to you? You call him Ernesto Leogrande? Is that he said his name is?"

"Vittorio Gelsi. The other name is—a joke. I know his name." Adam put the pictures on the officer's desk. "I want to help him. I am his friend."

"Pray for his wife, *Signore*. That will be most help."

"Well? Can I see him?"

"Not against his will, *Signore*. Prisoners have rights, too. He does not want to see you."

"He is embarrassed," said Adam. "I don't blame him. I still want to help him."

The officer shrugged. He smiled at Adam. "You can make a complaint if he has take your money."

"I don't want to make a complaint! Don't you see?"

"No." The *carabiniere* smiled again.

"If his wife is all right, will he be released?"

"He attempt murder, *Signore*."

Adam sighed. "I will go see his wife."

"*Sì, Signore*."

"I will do all I can for him," said Adam.

"That is not the business of the *questúra*," said the police officer.

The *questúra* was in an old palazzo in the center of Rome. The walls were khaki-colored, and there was an institutional atmosphere, brightened by the handsomely uniformed *carabinieri* stationed at the outer doors. As Adam came into the heat outside, he saw Dorothy taking pictures of the *carabinieri*. She smiled and waved at him, and it irritated him that she was not upset. At dinner last night, she had said she was just glad Ernesto had not gotten his hands on the money of the Fellow's Foundation. He had mentioned a building in Umbria to her, ideal, he had told her, for a headquarters for the Fellow's. The government would lease it for very little; there were just a few things to be repaired, and Ernesto had promised to get an estimate for the Fellow's, and handle the negotiations.

Adam had said, "But even if he is a crook, don't you feel something for him?"

"Sorry for him," had been her answer. "In fact, I'm going to speak about him at our next session."

Dorothy knew nothing about the $25,000 Ernesto had taken from Adam. Nor about the additional $15,000 he had failed to collect from Adam before his arrest. That money, plus $5000 more was all Adam had left, other than the $10,000 in the safety deposit box in South Orange, New Jersey.

When Dorothy saw Adam, she waved and called to him, snapping his picture as he walked toward her.

"Did you see him?"

"No."

"This isn't going to make you start drinking, I hope."

"No."

"I have to be back at the office in half an hour. Adam, I wish you'd visit Fellow's. Just to see it. Not join it. Just see it."

"I have things to do."

"No gifts, Adam. Please, don't send any more gifts to Venice."

"I didn't send *gifts!* I sent a gift. A baby-bib!"

"Returned."

"All right, they returned it. That was weeks ago, and it's all over. I don't mind telling you that I don't even think about Chary any more. Let her do as she pleases. I have too much on my mind now. A way to help Ernesto."

"You mean, Vittorio."

"Don't nag at me, Dorothy."

"Do you have something wrong with your eyes, Adam?"

"No."

"They look funny," she said. "Almost as though you were crying."

"Before I go to the hospital," said Adam, his head turned away from her so she could not see his eyes, "I'll stop by and pick up the mail at the apartment."

"Remember to call me if we hear from Shirley? I'm dying to know when she gets here."

"By now," said Adam, "she's probably dancing again."

Dorothy Schackleford was saying something about Shirley Spriggs having vowed not to dance for two years, and only one year was up, but for some reason, Adam was fighting back his tears with a greater urgency then, so that he was forced to cut short their conversation with the excuse that he needed a men's room, and that he would meet Dorothy at the Via Po apartment when she returned from work.

In the small *trattoría* where he found a men's room, Adam stayed to have lunch. He ordered *Zuppa di cozze,* and a mezzo-lítro of soáve. It was the first alcohol he had tasted since he had seen Billy and Chary, less than two months ago. Yesterday in Civitavecchia he had ordered a whisky in a place called Cucci's, but he had been unable to lift the glass, his hands were trembling so, his eyes filling with tears to a point where he felt people staring at him.

It was in Civitavecchia that he had finally begun to accept Ernesto's deception. Even after he saw Ernesto's picture in the paper, and went for the first time to the *questúra* to straighten out what he felt was an alarming case of mistaken identity, he was unconvinced that Ernesto had deceived him. He had gone to Civitavecchia a day later on the bus. As he rode along the old Via Aurelia, he smiled at the idea Ernesto had taken his money with no intention to ever build an Adamo's. Adamo's would be there, perhaps even finished (except for the air-conditioning, which he had never had the opportunity to pay Ernesto for). Despite Ernesto's wrongs, their dream of Adamo's in Civitavecchia was not among them.

There in Civitavecchia was the very building from the pictures Ernesto had shown Adam. Adam's heart had missed some beats at the sign: Cucci's . . . it was just remodeled, the waiter assured Adam, and Adam had sat out on the terrace waiting for his whisky, thinking of how often in his imagination he had sat on this same terrace, entertaining Luther Schneider, and Billy and Chary, laughing and talking on this same terrace. . . . Less than a week before he had come here to Civitavecchia, on one of Ernesto's and his walks through the Villa Borghese, Ernesto had told him that the terrace had been widened, that Adamo's would have the finest view of the sea in all Italy.

"You make me feel so happy, Ernesto," Adam had told him.

"Not *lèi*, Adam." Ernesto had seized Adam's wrist and pressed it with his palm. "*Tu*. We are friends. No longer *lèi*, but *tu*."

When the waiter brought Adam the whisky on the terrace at Cucci's, Adam had remembered Ernesto's touching invitation to Adam to use the familiar form of address. He had left the whisky and run off, and since then at odd times, Adam would find his eyes filling up, as they had a moment before coming to the *trattoría,* when he was leaving the questura with Dorothy.

Adam poured his wine and began to eat his mussels.

When he finished lunch he would visit Ernesto's wife in the hospital. He would reason with her. It would do her no good if Ernesto were to go to prison again.

Adam remembered what the waiter at Cucci's had said: "I come from these parts, *Signore*. There has never been a family named Leogrande, nor one named Gelsi who run the *pensione* you ask about. That name, both of them, I can tell you is not of anyone around here."

And in Adam's mind had come the retort: "Not yet, but wait!"

For there was still time, still some money left.

"*Tu*. We are friends," Ernesto had said, and Adam felt forgiveness was the only obstacle in their way now. Adam would forgive him all, just as Ernesto had tacitly forgiven Adam for a crime he would not even allow Adam to confess to him.

18

August 5

Dear Billy and Chary,

I am writing this after a visit to a friend's wife. I am upset because she is dead, and it will cause my friend a great deal of trouble. There is no point in going into it all, since we are so out of touch, and no longer seem to know the same people. However, I think of you often, even though we are not as close as we once were.

I am sorry that you did not like the baby's bib. I wish you had enclosed a note telling me what was wrong with it, as I want to exchange it for something you might like better. You are certainly hard people to buy gifts for! I never seem to get you something that pleases you.

Tonight from America a friend of Dorothy's is arriving named Shirley Spriggs. She is on her honeymoon with her husband Norman. This will keep us busy, but we always think of you two. I cannot tell you how happy I am that you are still married and everything is going well. I trust it is, or I would have heard otherwise. It is all right that you don't write because I know you are busy with the baby. Is it a boy, and if so, what did you name him? I am not fishing for compliments by that statement, because I can understand perfectly if you named him after either one of your fathers.

My best to both of you and continued good wishes for a happy marriage. My best also to Mrs. Cadwallader when you see her.

Yours,
Adam.

August 6

Tonia tells me you are bother at the hospital and everyplace, come even here to the *questura.* No money is owe you if you think that, and if you try to say there is money owe you, how do you prove? Stay away from my life.

Vittorio Gelsi.

August 8

Dear Billy and Chary,

I am writing this to you about Adam. He has started drinking again. He is very upset because a man who posed as his friend has turned out to be a crook, and now it seems, even a murderer. I do not want to bother you with this. I know you dislike Adam, and I can appreciate the reasons. It is just that lately I am worried about him to a point where I will do anything I can to help him. I believe he has practically exhausted his money from the sale of the *Stammbuch,* and I am not disinclined to think this crook also got some of that money. Adam mentioned once that he was in a hospital. This is what I am writing you about. I know he writes to you, and I know Billy talked with him a bit while you were both in Rome. Did he mention the hospital, or the doctor? Either or both would help me. Last night he called some florist in New York long distance and begged to have a charge account reinstated. I don't know what any of this means, but as you can see, things here are not so good. If you know anything that might help me find out the name of the hospital, I would be grateful.

Here at Fellow's we are set up to handle mental illness as well as other problems, but Adam will have nothing to do with the organization. I used to think he was simply an alcoholic, but sometimes I wonder. My best to you both, and forgive this intrusion, but it's necessary.
                              Dorothy Schackleford.

The *carabiniere* smiled at Adam. "All right, *Signore*. He has consent. You wait and in a moment, you can see him."

Adam went and sat on a straw-bottomed chair opposite the police officer's desk. He had not had a drink in twenty-four hours, not since the fight with Dorothy over the fact he had found her letter to Billy and Chary, opened it and destroyed it after he read it. Well, he had expected Dorothy to turn on him; it was just a matter of time. He supposed Shirley and Norman had triggered it, and as he waited to see Ernesto, he promised himself he would not return to the Via Po until they were out of Rome for good. Dorothy had made reservations down the street at the *pensione* for them, and for the past four days, the pair were forever intruding on Adam. Norman had even tried to talk to Adam "man-to-man", as Norman put it, about Adam's drinking. The whole apartment had taken on the atmosphere of The Salvation Army, and Adam was tired of it. Last night Adam had suggested Norman take Shirley dancing, which was the occasion for a crying jag on Shirley's part, intermixed with sniffling memories of Ginger Klein's demise, and a threat to punch Adam in the nose from Norman.

Norman had even had the gall to ask Adam what his intentions were toward Dorothy.

"What are hers toward me?" Adam had answered him. "To betray me to my best friends?"

The *carabiniere* signaled to Adam to follow him, while another officer took his place at the desk. Adam went behind the *carabiniere* up a dirty, badly-lighted staircase. At a dark passage, down a narrow corridor, the *carabiniere* took a key from a chain attached to his uniform, and unlocked a door. In this room, in front of another closed door, sat a young policeman with his cap perched sideways on his mass of black curly hair.

"Signor Gelsi," said the *carabiniere*.

He turned to Adam with another of his cryptic smiles. "Any time you want to sign a *denuncio*," he shrugged, "it might make you feel better, *Signore*." He tipped his hand to his cap, and walked out of the room. The policeman with the black curly hair pointed at a doorway, and Adam went inside. He sat on a bench and waited.

Friends come first, Adam thought, and he felt himself begin to choke up. When he saw Ernesto, he would say nothing about his shock at the knowledge that the woman in green from the whorehouse, was Ernesto's wife . . . nothing about Tonia, either, the brunette whore whom Adam had spent his time with, nothing about her angry denials that she had taken a thousand dollars from Ernesto to keep quiet about Adam. Another of Ernesto's lies, Tonia had insisted at the hospital, and Adam realized that one thing Ernesto had told him *was* true. All of his family did speak English; Tonia told him in very plain English that Ernesto had first intended to blackmail him. The meaning of her words, anyway, was very plain.

"You were afraid you say something to me, no? You didn't not say anything, but Vittorio know you afraid. He would have blackmail you, but you give him the money without he do it!"

Adam was able to figure it out, trace the whole thing from the day he handed Ernesto the thousand to keep the brunette quiet; in the next breath he had mentioned going into business with Ernesto. Then Ernesto had dropped the subject of the brunette and what she knew. If it had not been the club at Civitavecchia, it would simply have been more blackmail. Adam sucked hard on the Gauloise to keep himself from feeling very sad. Outside the room he heard the police officer exchange words with another policeman, then in the doorway, Ernesto stood.

"Ernesto!" Adam walked across to him smiling, while the policeman with the curly hair shut the door, staring at them through the wire window.

"Don't call me that. You know that is not my name." Ernesto was sober-faced, and Adam thought he even looked angry.

"I want to help you," said Adam.

Ernesto rubbed at his hook nose, and let his hand drop to his side again. "I come to tell you leave me alone, and leave my sister alone! Leave Tonia alone!"

"I only told her what I told you. I want to help you!"

"She does not want me to be helped!"

"Then forget her, Ernesto. We'll figure a way out!"

"There is no way. The best way is you go. Leave us all alone. I come to tell you that."

"I don't want the money back. You think that?"

Ernesto glared at him, arms akimbo, rocking on his heels. "What money?"

"You don't trust me. You think I care about the money. I don't!"

"You are crazy!"

"Sit down, Ernesto. I have an idea. Listen, we could still build the place in Civitavecchia. I was there, Ernesto. I saw the place, and we could still—"

"Don't call me that! You are crazy." He turned and said something to the policeman at the window of the door. Adam did not understand more than the word "open".

"I have so much to tell you," said Adam, "Please. We can talk. I could open the place in Civitavecchia and we could run it together when you are free. We could—"

Ernesto spat on the floor. The Italian policeman shouted something at him and began opening the door.

"I have never been to Civitavecchia," said Ernesto, "and I will never go now. I have seen pictures though," he laughed, a laugh of derision. "I have a friend who is a brick-layer. He just finished a place called Cucci's, a do-over job. Did you see Cucci's?"

"Why do you want to hurt me, Ernesto?"

Ernesto said something to the guard who stood in the doorway, and the guard returned the remark with another, and an obscene gesture. Both Ernesto and the guard laughed.

"I remember when you told me the things about man's inhumanity to man," Adam said. "I don't believe you want to be cruel."

Ernesto started walking toward the door. "I don't care what you believe. I have my life not to care. I have my life what is left to sit in a cell and do nothing but not to care what you believe!"

"Are you blaming me? Is that it?" Adam pulled at his arm. "Are you blaming me?"

"Without you, and your money there would have been no need to fight her."

Adam's eyes were filled with tears. "But I only wanted to——" He could not think any longer what it was he had wanted to do.

"To have your fancy club, ah?" said Ernesto.

"But it isn't my fault! I came here to help you!"

"Help yourself to a jump in the Tiber!" Ernesto said. He was in the entranceway of the room when Adam caught his arm a second time and held on to it. "Remember the day in the Borghese? Remember, you said I should say *tu*. Not *lèi,* you said. We are friends."

Ernesto shook his arm free. "Let go! Crazy!"

"*Tu,*" said Adam. "Ernesto, let me help you. Not *lèi,* you said, but *tu.*" The tears were starting down his cheeks. "Wait, Ernesto, there's so much more I want to say!"

Ernesto stopped and looked back over his shoulder at Adam.

There was a crooked grin on his face, and the silver medal around his neck gleamed against the dim light of the low-watt bulb overhead.

"At least I am not you," said Ernesto; "I am a man at least!"

He spat a second time and made the same obscene gesture which the policeman had made a moment ago. Then he turned his back on Adam.

19

"*. . . and this afternoon I am going to visit the grave of your wife. Do not be unhopeful about the future. In order to make it easier for Dorothy, who is entertaining friends from America, I will be at this hotel for a while. You may write me here, but* *if you don't I will understand that it is because they probably don't allow it. I know you did not intend to hurt my feelings during our visit. It is not an easy position you are in . . ."*

A LETTER FROM ADAM BLESSING TO VITTORIO GELSI

The hotel was on the Via Vittorio Emanuele Orlando, not far from the Mediterraneo. Adam was paying eight thousand lire for a double with bath, a deluxe rate, but he was glad to be away from the Via Po apartment. He posted the letter to Ernesto at the desk and walked out into a warm sunny day, not badly hung-over, not at all depressed. As he strolled along he looked for the familiar yellow sign with the telephone on it. There was one above a bar sign on the corner, and Adam ordered a whisky and asked the cashier for a *gettone* to make a call. He took his drink with him, dialed Dorothy's office number, and when she answered, Adam pressed the button to let the slug drop into the box.

"Where are you, Adam?"

"In a bar."

"Where are you staying, Adam?"

"The Holy Father has asked me to share his quarters in the Vatican."

"I don't appreciate that, Adam. I don't appreciate any of it."

"Did I get any mail?"

She let out a sarcastic little laugh. "Stacks of it, Adam, from all your friends. The florist in New York, the bartender in New York, Ernesto, Billy, Chary—I can't count all your mail."

"You're still mad, is that it?"

"Adam, I have to pay my phone bill. You called all over the world the other night. If Norman hadn't stopped you—"

"He's still around?"

"Of course he's still around. What do you think? Adam, he's a better friend than you know. They were supposed to go to Capri this week, and he's only staying because he's worried about you."

"I must be the most exciting thing that ever happened to Norman. Even more exciting than Shirley." Adam took a gulp from the whisky glass.

"Oh, Adam, you can't even stop drinking while you make a phone call. I can hear the glass."

"It's just wine."

"Norman was going to ask the police to help find you, if you didn't call today."

"The police have nothing on me," said Adam.

"Of course they haven't *got* anything on you! What kind of a way is that to talk! You were talking that way the other night! I don't know what you mean half the time any more! Adam, we're all very worried about you, that's all."

"I'm fine, Dorothy. Really. I really feel great!" He meant that. He felt tears in his eyes.

"Why don't you come back to the apartment?"

"When they go. Not before."

"Adam, I'll ask them not to stop by any more. Will you come back then?"

"It's the nagging I can't take," said Adam. "I haven't done such bad things." More tears. He turned his back on the bar so the old man behind it would not see his eyes.

"Where are you staying without luggage?"

"I have a new suitcase I bought."

"Oh, Adam, come back to the apartment."

"Yes," said Adam. "I want to. I want to pack everything."

"Pack?"

"I may have to go to Venice," said Adam. "Billy sounded worried the other night on the phone."

"Adam, he was worried about *you*."

"I know. I ought to reassure him."

"Come home, Adam, and we'll talk about it."

"You see, Dorothy," said Adam, "they could be having trouble with their marriage. They are some things you don't know, you see?"

"Adam . . . Just come home, will you?"

"I have to go to the Piazza Verano this afternoon. After that, maybe."

"The cemetery? Not the cemetery?"

"Ernesto's wife is there, Dorothy."

"What time are you going there?"

"Oh, after lunch, I suppose."

"All right, Adam."

"There's nothing to worry about," said Adam. "I just hate Norman."

"All right, Adam. I'll see you later then."

"Yes," Adam smiled. "Good-bye." He put the phone's arm back. There was a residue of tears in his eyes, which he brushed away with his fingertips. He swallowed the rest of his whisky and set off for the narrow old street north of Piazza Navona, the Via de Coronari.

The choice was between a silver salt cellar and an eighteenth century wood punch-ladle, with a worm handle and silver mounts. Adam stood in the antique shop trying to make up his mind. His book on silver was with the rest of his belongings on the Via Po, and while he was almost positive he would buy Luther Schneider the punch-ladle, he had some reservations. The punch-ladle was the more expensive gift, but the silver salt cellar was larger and looked less skimpy. Still, Schneider was more likely to have a salt cellar in his collection. Adam picked up one, then the other, ultimately choosing the punch-ladle. He left instructions for mailing, and enclosed the note he had written last night at the hotel. He had had to rewrite it this morning, for his hand had looked strangely unlike him, even though he allowed for the fact he was quite tight. It was a bewildering curiosity—last evening's handwriting sample. There were those odd breaks in the lower sections of his *a*'s and *o*'s. He had smiled to imagine such ominous traits in himself, and he had redone it with great care: "Greetings from The Eternal City with thanks for your faith in me." It was the first time he had ever put a message in with a gift for Schneider. He left it unsigned, but he felt a certain warm satisfaction at the thought that he had finally made a direct communication, as though somehow it gave more stature to his bond with Schneider. The clerk was smiling at Adam, bowing to him, being so very kind that Adam left the place with his eyes filled. There was a lot of good in the world, and as Adam crossed the street and headed toward the Piazza Navona, he realized he wanted to dine outdoors in the sun, where he could watch people, toast them with his wine in a secret sacrament, embracing absolute strangers and Billy, Chary, Ernesto . . . his friends. . . . He thought suddenly of the nice clerk from the Gracie Branch Post Office back in New York City, the one to whom he had handed over the change-of-address slip, and to whom he had told the fib about Chary's moving. The clerk had such a friendly face. When Adam had gone back to the post office to reroute Chary's mail the second time, he had looked for that clerk in vain. Adam wished he knew his name. He would have liked to send him a post card, even though the clerk would probably not know who it was from. He would simply have liked to send him greetings from Rome. Tears again. Adam blinked them away. He turned onto the Via Guiseppe Zanardelli, where he saw Passetto's, with the large summer terrace. He looked forward to a very happy luncheon there, and he had to stop a few feet from the entrance to get control of himself, to wipe his eyes.

A light rain began to fall as Adam was leaving Passetto's—a misty sort of precipitation with the sun still hot but screened by pinkish clouds. Adam had ordered an extra pot of coffee at the end of his meal, so that he no longer felt the gay euphoria he had while he was dining; instead, a not melancholy but more pensive feeling; serious, very serious now. A tonsured monk passed him in the street, and Adam crossed himself—the first time in his life he had ever done it, but it seemed very natural. In the taxi on his way to the Piazza Verano he remembered his first trip to Rome, when he had ridden an elevator to the roof of St. Peter's Basilica. There were bits of saints' bones for sale there, along with the rosaries, guidebooks and Benedictine liqueurs. There were signs everywhere which warned "Do not spit," and Adam had thought at the time that it was comical for such signs to be there, but now he knew that it was very sad and he understood those signs. They were not there because people would spit, Adam decided, they were simply reminders that at any time, in any place, man could turn on you and foul you. Who was safe really, where was anyone safe from unkindness or vulgarity? Adam

smiled. It no longer made him sad as it had in Passetto's
when he remembered Ernesto's last words to him; it made
him glad he could forgive Ernesto for another wrong, as
he had forgiven all his friends. Perhaps when he left the
cemetery he would return to St. Peter's and buy a small
sack of the saints' bones for Ernesto. Adam leaned back
and closed his eyes, his neck rubbing against the leather
seat, which was hot and sticky. He felt slightly dizzy,
and he wondered if he could give in to the impulse momentarily to let his mind whirl, as though it were a sep-
arate part unconnected with his body, and it would
whirl and spin, and even Adam would not be aware of
it . . . just for a few slow seconds. Like a weight lifted,
the end of great pressure . . . lightness, floating. Dancing.

"Signore! Per favore, Signore!"
Adam rubbed his eyes and sat up. The driver was
pointing to an ornate procession in front of them. Black
horses dressed in black plumes, a black hearse with a
man on top wearing a Napoleonic hat.
"Here you get out, *Signore!*" said the driver, with a
shrugging gesture to indicate his helplessness. "We are
sticked!" he said.
Adam paid him. He waved a hand in answer to the
driver's *"Grazie!"* and he walked along until he came to
the outside gates of the cemetery. The short nap on the
way had confused him slightly. He had the sensation of
having dreamed a horrendous nightmare, but none of it
could he remember. Just the feeling left from it—a pit in
his stomach; his heart beating too fast. He began to smell
the sickly odor of countless flowers which were set up
on stalls lining the cemetery's outer gates. He waited
while the black hearse passed through the gates; then he
bought a bunch of lilies and went in the direction of the
hearse.
Inside, the Piazza Verano was a world of marble, peo-
pled by marble angels, marble children, marble adults.
The living, like Adam, seemed to be intruders, and Adam
noticed that many of them walked in the careful, almost
apologetic manner of someone going through another person's house, without quite having his permission. Adam
passed a marble house in front of which two small mar-

ble boys dressed in sailor suits exchanged a living rose. An inscription on a stone beside them said they had lived from 1860 until 1870. They were brothers: Tullio and Giusto.

Adam walked on, and the rain was still the same vaporish quality, with the heat muggy, the sun pushing its fire through the veil of pink clouds. At another marble house, Adam saw a marble woman holding out her hand, as though she were beckoning to him. He stopped and stared at her. He imagined that he saw a faint smile on her marble lips. He looked beyond her and into the house. There were chairs to sit on. There was an altar with a white lace-edged cloth, and on the cloth were frames containing photographs of children. A bowl of oranges. A prayer book. Tiny lights burned under images of the Virgin.

Adam went closer to the marble woman, to read her name on the tablet, but there was no name. He looked up again at her face and then she seemed to frown. He turned his back on her and hurried away, and he realized as he passed house after house, he would probably never find Ernesto's wife's mausoleum. He was not even sure there would be one so soon; sure only that the newspapers had announced her burial in the Piazza Verano.

At a corner, mounted under glass on a small tombstone, was the photograph of a young boy about thirteen. He was posed standing on a hill with his arms pulling a dancing kite, his hair tossed in the wind, his face laughing. He wore knickers and a white blouse, and on one leg his stocking had slipped down to his ankles, and there was a dog pulling at the stocking. Under the photograph was a name—one word—followed with an exclamation point: Mario!

Adam walked across to the tombstone and placed the flowers there.

"Mario," he said. He smiled and bent close to the photograph, "Is that your dog?" There were tears starting in his eyes, but he did not fight them and they blurred; a drop fell on the photograph. "I didn't have a dog," he said. "Mario, I didn't have a dog."

Two priests passed with large soup-tureen hats, babbling together in Italian, smiling. They glanced at Adam and glanced away.

"I'll buy a kite for Timmy, Mario," Adam said. "I'll tell him about you."

Adam straightened and backed away from the small tombstone. He gave a little wave at the photograph, smiling, the tears on his cheeks. As he started around the corner and down toward some lights on the ground in the distance, he remembered something about the dream he had on the way to the cemetery. He had been caught running down a narrow street with a knife in his hand. He remembered he was wearing the foulard and damask-tie silk dressing gown he had bought for Billy's wedding gift. The smiling *carabiniere* from the *questúra* was arresting him for murder. He remembered that he had protested that he had murdered no one, and the *carabiniere* had only shrugged. "There is no reason, but it might make you feel better, *Signore!*"

Adam stopped at a wrought-iron grating in front of him. It fenced off row upon row of concrete slabs, a hundred or more, with small bulbs by each one. The bulbs were about fifteen watts, only a quarter of them burning. Near the gate sat a fat old man in a little house nearly too small for him, the size of a ticket window. Outside the house were more lights fixed to a central switchboard which the man operated, and which connected with the lights that circled the concrete squares.

Adam looked at the man, and the man said, "Five lire."

"Why?" asked Adam in Italian. Adam wiped the tears from his face with his handkerchief, while the man said in Italian, "For the dead."

Adam shook his head. "I don't speak Italian well."

The fat man shrugged. He did not speak English.

"Why?" Adam tried again.

Behind him a voice said, "The lights are for the people who rest here."

He turned and faced one of the priests with the soup-tureen hats. In the priest's hands was a rosary. He had great coarse peasant hands, and a gold tooth in front of his mouth. "I speak English," he said unnecessarily. "Did you lose someone?"

"Not here," Adam said. "I'm a visitor."

"This is the *ossario*. The people are buried here."

"Where?"

"In the *ossario*. Excuse me. In those wells." He pointed at the fenced-in area. "For the poor, *Signore*. This is where the poor rest. They cannot afford tombs and land is scarce in Rome, so we put them in the earth ten years. Then, when the time is up, the bones are dug up and they are buried here in a common grave."

Adam's eyes were blurred again from his tears. "Where are their friends who won't bury them?" he said. "Where?"

The priest looked at him a moment. Adam leaned into him. "Where are his friends?"

The priest stepped away from Adam. He was smiling. He said something to the fat man and the fat man shook his head and held his nose with his fingers. The priest nodded.

"I'm not drunk if you think that," said Adam.

"Perhaps not, *Signore*, but you have a smell of it."

The priest turned and moved away, handing the fat man some lire.

"Wait!" Adam called.

The priest turned, hanging back, and Adam hurried across to him.

"You have no right to treat me this way," said Adam.

"How did I treat you? I explained the *ossario* to you. I answered your questions."

"You told the man I was drunk."

"No," said the priest, "I said you had a liquor breath. No more."

"Why did you want to be unkind. You of all people! Isn't there enough unkindness in the world. Today at Passetto's I was snarled at because I accidentally knocked over a wine bottle, and now from a Father, this treatment!"

"*Signore*, I am a student priest, not a Father, and I have no time. Go back to your hotel and rest, *Signore*. Good day."

"Wait!" Adam said.

"Good day, *Signore*!" The priest walked fast, but Adam followed.

"Don't you know what's wrong? It's wrong to talk about people behind their backs!"

The priest did not look back. Adam continued following him. A woman kneeling by a marble statue of a nun looked up at Adam from her prayers, her rosary dangling in her hand.

Adam called to her: "He runs away from me! He is supposed to be a priest!"

"Listen!" Adam called after the priest. "I have a confession!"

He was hot and now slightly dizzy again. The priest was far ahead of him now, but again he shouted, "I have a confession to make to you. A crime! Wait!" He caught hold of a marble man, leaned on him, starting to sob. The rain was falling harder now. Adam stumbled as he moved on. He picked himself up again. The knees of his trousers were damp and dirty. The rain seemed to come more, and the pink color of the sky was turning to gray. Adam was very tired. He could not make it to the gates of the cemetery. He stopped again, and then again he saw the marble woman with her arms beckoning to him. He walked past her to the house behind her. His thirst was tremendous, and as he looked in through the window at the oranges on the altar, he thought of biting into one and sucking out the juice. When he tried the door, he found it locked.

"Please let me in," he whispered. He leaned his head against the door, felt the cool metal on his forehead. "Please let me in."

Behind him he heard someone shouting in Italian.

He let go of the door handle, and stumbled toward the marble woman. There was more shouting, and he saw people running toward him, people he seemed to recognize, but it was all a dream, wasn't it? He thought he heard Dorothy Schackleford's voice, but he fell to his knees without knowing if this were true. He put his head down on the cold marble slab beside the marble woman. "You don't have any name," he said to the cold marble. Then he toppled over on his back in the wetness, his eyes barely able to see the marble woman's face through his tears. He blinked his eyes and looked up at the face, and there were no features there, just as there was no name on the slab beneath her.

"And a lot you care!" said the marble woman.

EPILOGUE

THE FELLOW'S FLYER

Fellow's Foundation, Rome Chapter

Amid the festivity of the Christmas Season, we pause to note with reluctance and sadness, that we are losing one of our most valuable and diligent Fellow's workers. Adam Blessing is sailing for New York on the "Leonardo da Vinci," December 19th. Our questions as to his future plans were answered in typical Adam fashion, with the simple and profound sentence: "My future is in the hands of Faith."

Adam Blessing has been with Fellow's a year in January, heading up our Alcoholics Anonymous Chapter. No one who has ever heard "our Adam" speak, can doubt how sorely we will miss him. His accounts of his recovery from a mental illness were an inspiration to all—his confidence, his very nearly spiritual enthusiasm for his work, will make it utterly impossible for anyone to take his place. He can be succeeded—yes, but there is no one quite like "our Adam."

We have grown to think of him as our special "Blessing," and our Treasury will be in mourning for a long time (as all Fellow's members know by now, Adam was an unparalleled fund-raiser!). New Yorkers are in for a treat at the New Year's meeting of A.A., which will be an open meeting, and which "our Adam" will address. Remember the date well: January 30th, at 8:00 P.M. in Riverton Memorial Church on 5th Avenue and 90th Street.

We know Adam will be dropping in on another ex-Fellow's worker, Mrs. Wilson Neer, our own Dorothy Schackleford, who lives in Brooklyn Heights, New York. Dorothy was one of our leading lights for two years, heading up the Fellow's Children Center. Her cheerful smile and her hardy determination have been very much missed by all of us.

So, with our hearts full and our spirits inspired by Adam, we say *"Buon Natale,"* but never good-bye. And speaking for all of us, I would like to put it in a more personal vein . . . as Santayana once wrote: "I scarce know which part my greater be,/ What I keep of you, or you rob from me."

PART THREE

20

WIN WINS ROUND ONE THOUSAND-AND-ONE; Manufacturer Ordered Out—For Peace

A temporary cessation of hostilities was arranged yesterday as wealthy manufacturer Luther V. Schneider agreed to move out of the Bucks County estate he has been occupying with estranged wife Win Griswold Schneider, former society beauty.

Lawyers for both sides in this knock-down-drag-out litigation agreed with Supreme Court Justice Paul Lindgren, that the battle line should be drawn back. Win and her millionaire husband have been living in the same $99,000 mansion on Lerch Road, Point Pleasant, Pennsylvania, and concentrating too much fire power in one area.

Schneider, who claims his wife's romance with the bottom of the bottle is jeopardizing their son's health, has agreed to move into the family apartment on East 91st Street in New York, temporarily. Win, who claims any diversion she might have, nowhere near matches Schneider's romance with his $100-a-week private secretary, is suing Schneider for separation. She asked $8000 monthly alimony, but agreed to accept $600 a week temporary alimony while regrouping her forces. Meanwhile, she will have full custody of the boy, Timothy Schneider, 11. Some two years ago this boy was the victim of a kidnapper, who has never been apprehended, largely due to the fact that Mr. Schneider refused to cooperate with authorities. The ransom money was given over to the kidnapper with no identifying marks on any of the bills, which reportedly added up to $100,000.

In Schneider's counter-affidavit he claimed his wife, at the time of the kidnapping, was concerned more about the amount of the ransom than about the safe return of her son. Schneider attributed the safe return to the fact he did not cooperate with local authorities or the F.B.I., but "trusted" the abductor. He does not trust his wife with their son, claiming she has often beaten the boy and ridiculed him for being "unbalanced."

Lindgren had adjourned Win's separation trial without setting a date. This was three months ago. Since that time, he said, Schneider's attorneys called him to report that Win had locked the child in a toolshed behind the house, in retaliation for "an unfounded conviction," that Schneider was seeing Kate Weeks, his secretary, after office hours. Win's lawyers yesterday responded that the boy liked to play in the toolshed and that Schneider had maliciously misconstrued the game to mislead the court. The lawyers for Win Schneider added that Schneider's "gallivanting" with Miss Weeks was no secret to anyone. They said that Schneider had attacked their client, blackening her eye.

After listening to both attorneys in yesterday's Winter Court Session, Lindgren decided that, for the sake of the child, an armistice must be arranged, with Schneider's move the first step.

"Hello," said the voice.
"Hello."
There was a pause. Luther Schneider turned his swivel chair slightly to the left, facing his office windows. He said again, "Hello?" He glanced across his desk at Matt

Flannery. "Do you think it's Timmy calling from the country?" he whispered, as though Flannery knew any better than he himself knew. Flannery shook his head. "Don't get your hopes up, Lute." He had a faint smile of encouragement on his face. Sometimes when Win was out of the house Mrs. MacGivern allowed Timmy to phone.

Schneider said again, "Hello? Timmy?"

"No, it's not Timmy, Mr. Schneider."

"Who is it?"

"I have something important to talk over with you. It'll take a little time."

"Who are you?" Schneider said.

"A friend."

"Oh." Schneider looked across the desk at Matt and shrugged. Then he said into the phone's mouthpiece. "Just what are you calling about?" . . . He was getting used to it. He had never realized before this litigation how many friends Win did not have. To date, six of her alleged friends had offered to make affidavits on his behalf. There was a small matter of money involved, naturally. Some of the other calls making the same offers were from former servants. Win had never had a way with the help, unless it was a way of turning even the most docile, third-floor, three-day-a-week servant into a raging, indignant threatening human soul, who quit only after the most unbelievable anathemas directed at Win. Three weeks ago a chauffeur in their employment for a year and a half, had called Schneider to offer to testify "free-of-charge, sir, that the bitch would as soon see your kid dead as see the sun come up the next morning."

The voice on the telephone said: "You needn't sound angry. You did a favor for me, and I want to repay you, that's all."

"You'd better get to the point," said Luther Schneider. "I'm busy right now."

"Oh, you're not alone? I want to talk with you when you're alone."

"Good luck then," said Schneider. He saw Matt frowning at him from across the desk. He put his hand over the mouthpiece. "What?" he asked Matt. Matt said not to entirely discourage him.

"Can you call me later?" said Schneider to the telephone.

"Oh yes. I'm very patient, so don't worry."

"Try me in an hour," said Schneider.

He heard the click, the line went dead, and then the dial tone, and he set the phone arm back in its cradle.

"Another offer to defame the good character of your charming wife, hmm?" Matt Flannery blew on his glasses and wiped them with a corner of his handkerchief. "I wonder if *she* gets many offers."

"Probably thousands."

"Let's hope not one."

Flannery put his glasses back on. He picked up the thin onion sheets in front of him, leafing through them. "I'm on page 13, Lute, section 4."

Luther Schneider leaned back in his swivel chair, fondling his pipe while his lawyer began. "Section Four. On page 32 of her affidavit, Plaintiff states she was struck repeatedly by defendant on the night of September 16, and submits a doctor's report describing—"

Her neck. Schneider brushed a large hand through his gray hair and sighed. He had come close to strangling her that night. He had found her feeding Timmy whisky on a teaspoon to put him to sleep. A teaspoon won't hurt, she had said. Timmy was screaming, his face lobster-color; a teaspoon won't hurt his crazy head, for Christ's sake, she had said, falling in her drunkenness across Timmy.

"and vigorously deny that Plaintiff threatened her life then or at any other time," Matt Flannery continued, "and that pursuant to Section 309 of the Civil Practice Act—"

Luther Schneider remembered the Christmas a year ago, trimming the tree with Timmy downstairs. Win had come from upstairs, holding the whisky bottle by the neck, singing "I've Got A Lovely Bunch of Coconuts"— funny, how the mind remembered even the smallest details, like the song she sang then, and how he had stepped on a silvery-blue bulb on his way to her, trying to get her out of Timmy's sight before he saw she was naked. She wanted to know what the hell crazy kids knew about naked women anyway. "You're his mother—" yelling it; and Win yelling back just as loud: "I didn't give birth to that monster!" . . . "I'll kill you," he had said. Going around and around on the victrola—the Christmas carols: *Holy infant, mother and child*; Yes, I'll kill you, he had said. She laughed at him: "So you can be with her, Lute! Spawn another creep with her?" . . . Timmy watching everything, dressed in a pair of one-piece pajamas, standing under the tree: *Sleep in heavenly peace*.

Schneider only half-listened to Matt Flannery. He shut his eyes as though with that motion he could shut out the pictures in his mind's eye as well, the thousand snapshots there—the rewards, the punishments, take your choice; Kate leaning over in the morning to put her bra on, something that simple, recorded as well as Win in a rage at the doctor, the year Timmy was three and they knew for certain he was unbalanced, the blue vein that stuck out in her neck and her screaming: "The hospital gave us the wrong goddam baby, and you send this idiot back and tell them to find out where ours is!" . . . Kate and Timmy walking ahead of him the day they all went to the Central Park Zoo, the sudden sight of Timmy skipping, holding to Kate's hand . . . as well as Timmy hiding behind the shower curtain in the upstairs bathroom of the house in Bucks County, five o'clock in the afternoon when Luther Schneider had come home early; telling Timmy, no, son, Mommy isn't after you with a knife. You dreamed it, son . . . lying to him . . . Schneider opened his eyes and looked across at Matt.

"I didn't hear you, Matt."

"I said, 'That's it.' Of course, I don't think any of it will stop Win or her lawyers, but it might impress the court, the parts about her mistreatment of Tim anyway . . . that's what we really want. Tim!"

Luther Schneider said, "For the time being, that's all. I'm going to marry Kate, Matt."

"First things first, Lute. Watch that damn temper of yours, if you want my opinion." Matt was stuffing papers into his briefcase, removing his glasses, and rubbing his eyes. "I mean it. Don't knock her around any more. Hell, you know I'd like to help you knock Win from here to the Battery, but it doesn't show up well in court, Lute."

"I don't want to knock her anywhere." Luther Schneider sighed.

"I know. She practically begs you to slug her. I know that. It's better you're apart for a while. Mrs. MacGivern will look out for Tim."

"I'm not really worried for the time being about him."

"Mrs. MacGivern's good with him, Lute."

"I know. She can handle Win when she has to, too."

Flannery got his overcoat from the leather couch in Schneider's office. "I'll be glad when Kate gets back here and things are normal again. I liked the way she used to take care of me. Get me into this thing and all," said Matt, sticking an arm in his overcoat sleeve. "She still in Bermuda?"

"Yes."

"A wonderful girl," said Flannery. "And that's an unqualified endorsement." He smiled and shook Schneider's hand, saying, "I know it's unsolicited too, but I like her Lute, for the record, hmm?"

"Thanks," Schneider said.

"It's starting to snow out. Better not stay late." He waved and started out the door. Before it shut, he said, "Let me know if anything comes of that phone call, hear?"

"Another bum steer, probably," Schneider said.

Still, he waited at his desk for the telephone to ring. He was in the middle of a letter to Kate Weeks when the operator signaled an incoming outside call. He had made a rule that all incoming-outsides be put through on a direct wire. Matt's suggestion. Operators intimidate the real leads along with the phonies, Matt had said; we can't pick and choose; have to hear them all.

The voice said, "Can we talk privately for a while now?"

"Yes."

"I read in the papers about the troubles you've been having. I know you have to take precautions. Your wire could be tapped, I suppose."

Schneider said, "No melodramatics, hmmm? My wire is not tapped. Just get on with it."

"I'm sorry about all your trouble. I would have come home earlier if I had known. I read about it in Rome."

"Rome!" Schneider said.

"Oh, I know it wasn't in the foreign press. I got some back newspapers from another American. Scandal sheets, you know."

"And?"

"And I came home."

"Just to help me, hmm?"

"Yes."

"I see." Schneider shook his head and sighed, swinging his chair around to face the window and watch the snow falling.

"I'm sorry about all your trouble. Your wife has been very unkind. I hate unkindness."

"Are you a former friend of Win's or a former servant?" said Schneider.

"I'm your friend."

"Yes, of course . . . of course. Granted that, how did you know Win?"

"I didn't. I only saw her once. On the street. Near your place on Ninety-first."

"What is it you want Mr.—Mr.—"

"You wouldn't know my name, Mr. Schneider. I thought by now you might have guessed who I am."

Schneider rubbed his forehead with the palm of his left hand, an expression of exasperation on his lean countenance. "Well, I didn't guess. I'm sorry. I'm not good at guessing."

"I sent Timmy a tiny Basque fishing boat from Biarritz. I think that was the first gift. Oh, I know it's presumptuous to use the word gift—" Schneider's eyes grew wide with amazement as he leaned forward, holding the phone even closer to his ear, as though it was impossible to believe what he was hearing. The Basque fishing boat from Biarritz, the cock-eyed red sail attached to it. It had arrived that fall when Win was having another of her "rests" at the Hartford Retreat. Schneider had made a note to ask her who they knew who might be vacationing in southern France. It had slipped his mind to ask her; the gift had been passed along to Timmy with no special significance attached to it. . . . It had taken Luther Schneider over a year to put the puzzle together; another gift from Paris—this one for him, the helmet-shaped silver cream jug. They had both been sent to the Ninety-first Street apartment. The jug he had not taken with him to the country. He had not mentioned it to Win either. It had arrived shortly after she had found out about Kate, and everything that arrived was reason for suspicion, every Christmas gift, birthday gift, letter, bill —it was nearly the worst period of their marriage. He had left it with the rest of his silver. . . . There was a food broker—Saperstein, or Sardonspore—some name like that, for whom he had once done a favor. Schneider had heard he was in Europe for General Foods. Perhaps he was the donor, Schneider had thought, but it was an unconvincing explanation. The jug was very expensive, well over $600. . . . The piece in the puzzle, which Schneider needed to solve the matter, arrived from Rome. The punch-ladle; the card with "greetings" and "thanks for your faith in me." . . . Then he knew. The silver salt spoons, the Basque cap for Timmy, the miniature Vatican City Swiss Guard—he knew who had sent all of them. Win would have had a lot of satisfaction in the knowledge that Timmy's kidnapper was again in touch with Schneider. She was the main one to say he would hear from him again. When Schneider had paid the ransom, it was Win in her shrill tones who promised: "This is just the beginning of what you're going to pay that fellow!"

". . . none of the gifts would have been possible without your trust in me," the voice was saying, "and now I'm going to pay you back."

"You're going to *what*?"

"Repay you, Mr. Schneider. It was always my dream to repay you."

Schneider sat back against the leather swivel chair. "Repay me?" he said incredulously. He had not told anyone about the gifts being sent him. Against everyone's advice—Win's, of course—but also Matt's, his mother's, the F.B.I. agent's—against everyone's, he had kept his bargain with the kidnapper. He had purposely framed his response to the ransom note in a way intended to convince Timmy's abductor he would not turn on him. He had used words like "faith" and "integrity," appealing to him in a soft key, trying to reach him on whatever substrata level there was in his make-up which would respond to another human being's confidence in him. At the time he had thought of it as being like attempting to get some very fragile and infinitely precious object from the sticky hands of a recalcitrant child, approaching him inch-by-inch on tip-toe, afraid that one false move would send the object flying to destruction. . . . He had tried to be ever so careful, and in the same way one does not ever fool some children, he had not tried to fool the man who had Timmy captive. . . . And it had worked. He had never regretted the way he had handled it. Long afterwards, when he realized it was this same fellow sending the gifts from abroad, his reasons for telling no one were striped half with fear that it would start a resurgence, half with a thin acceptance of the idea that the kidnapper felt remorse, gratitude, guilt—Schneider did not know what to call it. There was an ocean separating them. Schneider had simply let well enough alone. . . . He had not even told Kate about it, and he told Kate nearly everything, omitting only the raw details of his life in hell with Win. He was not a superstitious man, Luther Schneider, but he felt there was something frangible about the understanding which had passed between himself and the kidnapper, something that must keep it a covert thing; almost as though after all the time that had passed, if Schneider were to break his word, what would stop the kidnapper from finding some way to retaliate; this time, to harm Timmy? . . . Now he could only repeat his last words, "Repay me?" as though the most disbelieving, lip-service Catholic had suddenly been confronted with the vision of St. Peter saying: "You have kept faith and now I am here."

"Yes, that's right, Mr. Schneider. Where will you be, for example, tomorrow?"

"That's New Year's Eve," said Schneider.

"A perfect time to settle old debts, isn't it, sir?"

"I usually go to my mother's for the day *and* evening."

"Good. Tradition is a fine thing. I believe in tradition myself."

"Is this a joke? I have trouble believing this is—"

The voice laughed, "No, you have never had trouble believing. You believed in me sir. You never gave me away. You gave me great peace."

"I'm—gl-glad," Schneider managed.

"You sound as though you doubt me. I don't blame you. I'm sorry I cannot see you in person to thank you.

I would like to shake your hand, Mr. Schneider. Thanks to you, I have been many places and seen many things. It has not all been easy for me; I have suffered too, and caused unhappiness to others. But I found my way finally. A whole new world opened up for me. A new field."

"A profitable field too," Schneider said. "It must be very profitable if you really mean that you're going to pay me back."

"It's not something I can explain on a telephone. Even in person, I wonder if I could explain it. It's very involved, you see."

"You got into some line abroad?" Schneider imagined telling Matt this. Matt was a lawyer first, of course. He could hear Matt's answer. "The man broke the law, Lute, and you didn't report his contact with you. You're an accessory! I don't care if he did pay you back!" Schneider was smiling all the more. Matt would damn near die once he got over being a lawyer.

"Yes, abroad. In Rome. It started in Rome, really."

"I see. . . . Well, Mr.—I don't know what to call you. Mr.—"

"I would tell you my name if I were sure you completely trusted me. Oh, I know you used to. When you had a reason to, you had faith. But you see, it's a funny thing about faith. Unless there is a good reason, one loses it."

"You're quite a philosopher."

"You've accomplished that for me. All my life I needed just one person to trust me. You did."

Schneider could think of nothing to say. He watched the snow. He could not stop imagining the look on Matt's face when he told him about this. Still, he could not quite believe it yet.

"I would like to tell you so many things," the voice said. "I can't. The things that have happened to me one doesn't sit down and discuss." There was a pause; Schneider heard a long sigh, then: "I will repay you tomorrow night."

"How do you intend to do this?"

"I can't say how. I wish I could. How or where, I can't

say, but you will be paid in full. I can promise that. By midnight."

"My mother," Schneider said, "is very old. She has a weak heart. I—"

The voice cut in: "Don't worry. I won't be anywhere near your mother's."

Matt was picking Timmy up tomorrow morning, bringing him to Schneider's mother's home on Gramercy Park. Visiting privileges; Schneider thought they were the most sadistic words he had ever heard in any court. . . . The voice was reassuring him again; don't worry, it would be managed efficiently; no embarrassment to anyone. Schneider played with his pipe as he listened; thank you, the voice was saying again, and then again the part about having always dreamed of repaying him. Always. Thank you.

Schneider straightened up in his chair. "I want you to understand something," he said, "If this is any sort of joke, or trick, or an attempt to get more—"

"Please! Please!"

"Well, I want you to be damn sure I'm not putting up with anything else! Do you understand!"

"I forgive you for looking at it that way. How could you look at it any other way? I forgive you!"

"Thanks."

"Please, before I say good-bye, I'd like to hear a kinder tone. I know that's very brazen of me. After all, I have no reason to expect kindness from you, but I've grown to think of you as my friend. I've thought of you more or less as my benefactor. That's the word, all right—my benefactor."

Schneider said, "Happy New Year! Will that do?"

"Your tone sounds harsh still. Do you mean it?"

"If you mean what you're saying," said Schneider, "I mean what I'm saying."

"I swear by God," the voice said. "I swear it!"

Then before Schneider could think of a rejoinder, the voice said, "Good-bye, Mr. Schneider. You'll never hear from me again, but I'll never forget you. I like to think you'll never forget me."

"Maybe I won't," Luther Schneider said; and, as he heard the receiver click, he thought: maybe I really won't, and he had the same feeling he had had the night before Timmy's return, a certain blind confidence in something all the odds were against happening; almost like a rapport with a perfect stranger . . . and yet a stranger who knew better than Luther Schneider's most intimate friends, that the one thing Schneider had always wanted was an eighteenth century punch-ladle with a worm handle and silver mounts.

21

The Fellow's Foundation
240 Park Avenue
New York, New York

Dear Sirs:

At the request of an anonymous donor, we have been directed to present the New York Chapter of the Fellow's Foundation with the following check for $10,000. The donor specified that the announcement of this gift be made known at the open meeting of the Fellow's Alcoholics Anonymous Meeting on January 30th at 8:00 P.M. A certified check for that amount is attached to this letter.

Sincerely yours,
A. K. Beardsley, Vice-President,
South Orange Savings and Trust Company
South Orange, New Jersey.

"He wasn't that fat when I knew him," said Dorothy Schackleford Neer.

"So that's the great Adam," her husband said. He giggled, and a woman in the row in front of him turned around in her seat and damned him with her eyes. A hiss of "Shhh!" spread through the audience.

"Well, he wasn't!" said Dorothy Schackleford in a peeved whisper.

She had always made more of her friendship with Adam. She was always telling Wilson how she had nursed Adam through his breakdown, helped him become interested in the Fellow's Foundation, watched him progress from a wild ne'er-do-well to a dedicated worker, and ultimately parted from him, with a little Schackleford embroidery on the latter. Well, he *might* have asked her to marry him—it wasn't exactly a proven lie. . . . Wilson was a few inches shorter than Dorothy, and without his glasses he could not see his own nose, but Dorothy thought of him as "a dear thing," and she was proud of the fact that he was one of the top engineers in Duco Oil Corporation. In April, they were going to Sumatra to live.

The speaker who had announced the $10,000 donation was pounding on the podium for order. There would be a hush momentarily, then a resurgence of the applause and chatter. The audience was as excited by the donation as they might have been if it were to be distributed among them in hundred-dollar bills. Behind the speaker, Adam stood, waiting to address the audience. He was enormous, Dorothy could not deny that. She wondered rather unkindly where on earth he bought his clothes, or did he have to have them made. His beard was even longer than it had been when she last saw him in Rome, and he looked much older than twenty-six.

Wilson leaned over and said: "He should have come a week earlier. He would have been the Santa Claus at the Christmas Party."

"*Wil*-son!" . . . but she was not truly angry at the remark. She just hoped Wilson would be nice after the meeting when he met Adam. Wilson was not what Dorothy would describe as a sensitive person. She always thought engineers were not the type to be sensitive anyway. They were all slide rules and fix-things-down-in-the-basement. Once she had told Wilson how Adam had attempted to kill himself, after that Vittorio Gelsi's execution. She had tried to explain to Wilson that Adam felt responsible, even though he was not in the least responsible. For a while Adam had even believed *he* had murdered Gelsi's wife, and he had gone about saying he must repent. Bats in the belfry, Wilson had said, marbles in the attic, but that was Wilson for you.

The audience was quiet now, and Adam was stepping up to the podium.

"I thought you said he was such a sporty dresser," Wilson whispered.

"Well, he was!"

The knees of Adam's pants were baggy, and there was no press in his suit. Worse, he wore a yellow shirt with a crooked green tie. Dorothy wished she had left Wilson home.

Adam had a hand on either side of the podium. He was leaning forward, staring out at the audience, waiting for silence. Finally, after several slow seconds in this pose, he straightened. His face was very grave, and when he spoke, his voice boomed out in the small church basement.

"My name is Adam Blessing. I am an alcoholic."

He paused and again looked at the audience. Dorothy attempted a faint smile when he looked in her direction, but if he recognized her, he showed no sign.

He said, "I used to hide behind a bottle for courage. I am not going to stand here and lie to you, and say I did not find the courage I needed, because I DID find it. I had a GREAT DEAL of courage when I drank. Drink gave me courage to pursue a very beautiful girl . . . My best friend's girl." There was a sprinkle of laughter from the audience. Adam Blessing waited for it to subside.

He began again, "Drink gave me courage to propose marriage to this girl. . . . Today, I am still a single man."

More laughter.

"I am also minus one best friend."

Laughter again.

"He was proposing all over the place," said Wilson.

"He exaggerates," Dorothy whispered back.

"Oh sure," Wilson said, "you were the only girl he ever proposed to, I suppose."

"Drink," Adam boomed out, "gave me the courage to behave as a rich man, when I was a poor man, gave me debts when I was debt-free, gave me the courage to be a thief when I was honest. There is an awful lot of courage in a fifth of whisky!"

Applause.

Adam Blessing's eyes were narrowed, now as he resumed: "Courage is defined as that quality of the mind which enables one to meet danger and difficulties with firmness. Dangers and difficulties, friends and Fellow's, not delusions of dangers and difficulties, not imaginary dangers and difficulties, but real ones. Liquid courage, the kind you find in a fifth of whisky, is one of the best manufacturers of synthetic difficulties and dangers in the world today! Is there courage in a fifth, oh yes, and plenty of it, but it's liquid!"

More applause. "Words, words, words," said Wilson. "I like it better when girls speak and tell how they almost undressed in public when they were drinking."

Adam Blessing said, "Some of us are people with little courage. If we are alcoholics, we need to supplement our threads of courage with faith. How do you have faith? Faith is contagious. You believe in me, and I'll believe in you. We members of Alcoholics Anonymous have demonstrated that credo to the fullest degree. I once looked up 'Faith' in the dictionary. I found it defined as 'fidelity to one's promises.' Of course! Fidelity to one's promises! You trust me and I shall trust you. I will not ever forget you. If it seems as though I am letting you down, it is not so. You are on my mind constantly. It is just a matter of time before I will be with you again. Faith!"

"What the devil is he talking about?" Wilson asked his wife. Some of the audience were looking at one another with puzzled expressions. Dorothy Schackleford Neer smiled, half with embarrassment, half with amusement. Adam used to be called "The Preacher" in Rome when he first began with Fellow's.

"I will leave you, but I will be back."

"A tiny nosegay to General MacArthur," Wilson snickered.

"You are always on my mind!"

"He would have been a great song-writer in the thirties," said Wilson.

"Tonight," Adam Blessing roared, "we heard of a donation of $10,000 to the New York Fellow's Chapter. What pure joy for the donor! Give, and you will be blessed!"

A few members of the audience were stifling smiles. There was a buzz of exchanged comments, shoulders shrugging with bemusement. Wilson gave his wife a questioning glance. "Is he all right?"

"He's just not organized," said Dorothy Schackleford, but she hoped he would not go on much longer. She glanced at her watch. The audience was very noisy now.

"Money cannot bring you peace, that is my message. Give it away! Peace is infidelity to one's promises, in the returning of another's faith in you, in the thought— no, the CONVICTION that faith can make you do ANY- THING! Love, MURDER, cry, laugh—"

"He looks like he's really crying himself," Wilson said.

"Oh God, I'm afraid he is."

"He is?"

"He needs a rest." Dorothy Schackleford covered her eyes with her hands, so she would not have to look at Adam.

Afterwards, he seemed all right. The chairman had interrupted him five or six minutes after Dorothy had stopped watching the podium. The chairman had said something about the meeting running overtime, and Adam, with the tears wet on his cheeks, had stepped aside without a protest. Dorothy and Wilson went up to him, and Adam hugged her with enthusiasm and shook Wilson's hand solemnly. They adjourned to a Schrafft's on Madison Avenue. Adam consumed two chocolate sundaes, and a piece of coconut layer cake. He asked Wilson about his work, and reminisced with Dorothy about members of the Fellow's in Rome. They were very nearly ready to leave when he brought up the names of Billy and Chary.

"Of course, I didn't expect a card at Christmas," he said, "but then again it might have arrived after I left. I might not have it yet."

"They're in Caracas," said Dorothy. "Billy's head of the Caracas office. We got a brief note from Chary on the back of their Christmas card. She's going to have another child."

"Caracas," Adam repeated.

"City of American-sponsored laundromats," said Wilson facetiously.

Adam seemed not to hear him.

He was playing with the cake crumbs on his plate, pushing them about with his fork. "I never knew what they named their boy."

"Ted."

"Oh . . . Theodore."

"Teddy, Chary calls him."

"I guess they didn't name him after anyone."

Dorothy could see the tears forming in Adam's eyes again.

She said, "What will you do now, Adam?"

"I've saved some money. I imagine I'll rest awhile."

"Good!"

"Rest, and eventually settle down somewhere," Adam said after the pause. "I have something to finish up here, and then—I'll settle down somewhere."

Dorothy picked up her gloves from the table. "It was good to see you again." Then she braved, "We liked your talk."

"I get worked up sometimes," Adam said softly. "It's as though everything builds up in me with such an urgency, I nearly explode."

"We better get on, Dorothy." Wilson was pushing back his chair.

"In Rome," said Adam, "I realized there was an obligation I must fulfill immediately. It upset me, the realization, but it brought me peace too. Perhaps it is the only true thing I'll ever do."

"Oh, you've done a lot of good in Rome, Adam. I heard all about it!"

"I'm very tired. Very tired . . . I'd like to settle down."

"We're walking as far as the subway, Adam."

"Go along. I'll have a glass of milk I think. Good night, Wilson."

"I love your beard, Adam." Dorothy was standing facing him, not quite sure the evening should end so flatly. But Wilson had made it very clear: *for the love of Pete, don't ask him back to the place!*

Adam said, "I'm going to shave it off tonight." He smiled. "It gets caught in the steering wheel."

"You have a car, Adam?" She could hear Wilson sighing behind her.

"I learned to drive in Rome, a month ago. I thought I might rent a car and practice."

She took his hand. "Good-bye, Adam. Let us hear from you."

"Good-bye and Happy New Year," he said. He dropped her hand and smiled. "It's nice, isn't it," he said, "to begin all over again?"

22

NOTICE

At three p. m. Mr. Blessing will visit The William Penn Lounge for another session in graphology. First Class Passengers only. On Tuesday and Thursday, he will be available at the same time in Lounge 2, for Tourist Passengers.

S.S. Quaker City
Philadelphia Line

Mr. Arlington Partidge of Rochester, New York, asked Mrs. Arlington Partidge if she was falling for that fat, phony slob or what?

"I'll be back in a minute," she answered, handing him her shuffleboard mallet. I just want to ask him one thing, Arl!"

She left her husband behind and hurried across to the deck rail where Mr. Blessing was standing, his arms behind his back, watching the sea.

"Hello there, Mr. Blessing." There was something almost saint-like about him, Mrs. Arlington Partidge often thought, and she did not mind it somehow that he showed no interest in who had spoken, but simply stayed in the same stance, touching his hand to his forehead in a slight salute, without looking to see who it was he was greeting.

"It's Mrs. Partidge," said Mrs. Partidge, "Ethel Partidge, remember? My *t*-bars tend to slant downward, and I have those broad *r*'s, remember?"

Mr. Blessing looked down at her. "Yes, I remember. You had very large handwriting, too."

"You really are something, Mr. Blessing! Memory like an elephant," she said. She thought when she said it that it was rather an unfortunate comparison. Mr. Blessing was so huge. "Yes, and you said I was an extrovert! Arl, my husband, tells me if I join just one more committee, he's going to wring my neck. I'm always doing sum'thin!"

"It is good to serve."

"Mr. Blessing, I feel like you know *all* my secrets. I mean, when you said that about my *m*, about the last stroke of my *m*, remember?"

"The fact that it was more angular than the other?"

"Wow-boy! You do remember everything! Well, yes, that's what I mean. I mean, I doubt that my own husband knows I'm a little neurotic."

"Mrs. Partidge, I did not say you were a little neurotic. I said it could be a sign of that, or it could simply indicate a desire for self-assertion."

"I mean, what would *you* think of a woman who sits around wondering what it would be like to have dinner with Dave Garroway. I don't mean just wonder, either, I mean set the table in my mind and everything, right down to what color linen napkins. Now!"

Mr. Blessing said, "I don't know who Dave Garroway is, Mrs. Partidge, and anyway, I really can't talk now. I'm thinking."

"Lord, you mean you're analyzing in your mind? I interrupted you analyzing in your mind?"

"It's quite all right. It was a brief interruption."

"Forgive me, Mr. Blessing. I'll just run right along and not bother you with another word. I had no idea you were doing *that*. Please excuse me."

At dinner that night Mrs. Partidge told Claire

Cottersley-Smith how she had come upon Mr. Blessing that afternoon when he was analyzing in his mind. Claire Cottersley-Smith said that was nothing, wait until she told Ethel what Al had to say when he got back to their stateroom last night. Claire said, "Al said, 'well, I had a talk with your boyfriend, Claire,' and Al said they stood on deck for nearly twenty minutes passing the time of day. Al said his guess was Mr. Blessing was a defrocked priest. Mr. Blessing talked a great deal about Rome, Al said, and Al said Mr. Blessing had a misty look in his eye."

"Well, that's the very same look we've seen two or three times. Like he was crying!"

"Exactly," said Claire Cottersley-Smith, "and if you ask me Al is right. Ever notice how he avoids women? Well, he's shy! He was a priest, and he's not used to women!"

"He's like a man without a friend in the world," Ethel Partidge said. "It makes me want to die inside, does it you?"

"Yes," said Claire . . . "A *de*-frocked priest! Imagine! Reduced to fortune-telling on a cruise boat!"

"Graphology, Claire! It's more scientific. You should know what he told me about my *m*'s."

Claire Cottersley-Smith was more interested in Mr. Blessing than in Ethel Partidge's *m*'s. After the old Jerry Lewis movie in the William Penn Lounge, she nagged her husband into trying to have a second conversation with Mr. Blessing. "Ask him," she said, "if he knows Latin. That'll clinch it!"

She and Ethel Partidge nursed green Stingers in the bar with Arlington Partidge, who was slightly miffed at the fact Al Cottersley-Smith had established contact with the mysterious Mr. Blessing, and not he.

"One day your Mr. Blessing will simply drop dead of a heart attack," Mr. Arlington Partidge said. He was extremely thin, and he never allowed Ethel to say that he was skinny.

"I like a lot of meat on a man," Claire Cottersley-Smith said.

After both women had had a third green Stinger and were right at that point of giggling hilariously at anything Arlington Partidge said, as long as it was not funny, Al appeared.

"Not a priest," he said sitting down. "Order me a whisky."

"Why not a priest?" his wife said.

"Well, we were having this talk about people who take these cruises, see? I say people get along in years, kids grow up, get through college and all that, and folks decide to spend a little money on themselves for a change, go away, see some sights."

"Yes? Yes? Go on."

"I need a whisky . . . well, he says to me that it's too bad money is so important to people. He says to me it used to be important to him, but he found out it wasn't and then he says something I damn near died at." He signaled the waiter for a whisky.

"What?" said Claire and Ethel together.

"He said he came into a great deal of money only a few years ago. A great deal, he said, repeating it, you know, like it was a million dollars or something? Well, this is the part that kills me. . . . He said he gave it all away, every nickle of it except for a small amount he had already spent selfishly on himself. He said he gave it all away to a worthy charity, and then he found peace!"

On Wednesday Ethel Partidge reported to Claire Cottersley-Smith that in a brief conversation with Mr. Blessing she learned this was the first time he had ever worked on a cruise boat, that he was not going to do it after the boat docked, that he had no "regular line."

On Thursday Claire Cottersley-Smith reported to Ethel Partidge that Al said Mr. Blessing spoke with Al for a half an hour on Faith and Loyalty, and Al saw real tears in Mr. Blessing's eyes, and Al was back to his original belief that Mr. Blessing was some kind of defrocked priest.

"Al said he said he had once done a terrible thing, but it was a beautiful thing too because it was necessary and true."

"A woman!" Ethel Partidge said. "Oh, gaw, he got involved with a woman!"

"That's what I think and that's what Al thinks. He messed around with some woman!"

"What kind of woman would let a priest mess around with her? Would you?"

"I don't know," Ethel Partidge said. "I might . . . if it was one of those terrible passions, I might not be able to stop!"

"It'll haunt him the rest of his days. I told Al that at breakfast. The rest of his days."

"How come he said he'd found peace, if he got himself defrocked for messing around with a woman?"

That night Arlington Partidge came into dinner beaming like a Cheshire cat.

"You would all be interested in something that just happened to me," he said. "In the radio room."

"Oh, Arly, don't play games!"

"Your shipboard Romeo was writing a cablegram. I just happened to see it over his shoulder. I just happened," Arlington Partidge announced in a triumphant tone, "to jot down its contents."

Ethel, Al, and Claire all made a dive for the slip of paper he set on the center of the table.

ARRIVING SATURDAY ABOARD S.S. QUAKER CITY. MY WANDERING IS AT AN END. I AM READY TO SETTLE PERMANENTLY. NOT WITH YOU NECESSARILY, BUT NEAR YOU CERTAINLY, TO HELP YOU FOREVER IN ANY WAY I CAN. BRING BABY TO MEET BOAT. WE WILL ALL BE REUNITED AT LAST.

"A baby!" said Claire Partidge.

"Who did he send the cable to. Did you see her name?"

"No," Arlington Partidge said, "he had not filled that in when I saw it."

Friday was spent with Ethel and Claire sitting about on the shuffleboard deck, reconstructing how they imagined it had happened. Ethel favored the idea a young girl came to confess a slight sin to him, and he led her on to greater sin. Ethel said it could just as easily have happened to her, if she were single, say, and on this very cruise; it could just as easily have begun with her casual mention of her *m*'s to him, that day on deck when he was analyzing in his mind.

Claire favored the idea, that he had become involved with a fast whore, but she agreed with Claire that it most likely began in a confession box.

Arlington Partidge and Albert Cottersley-Smith, when asked their opinion, chorused that they were very nearly bored silly with the mere thought of Mr. Blessing, and on Friday night they stayed up long after their wives had gone to bed, drinking whisky and discussing the matter.

Saturday the S.S. "Quaker City" docked on time, on the dot of noon. Up until then the morning had been spent in frantic fashion by both the Partidges and the Cottersley-Smiths, who were not weathered travelers, and were anxious with thoughts of things they forgot to pack, mislaid passports, and the exchange of adieus and addresses with other passengers. They all decided to have a drink together at a bar near the wharf, as a farewell gesture, and it was while they were deciding on the bar to meet in that they got a last glimpse of Mr. Blessing.

"Look!" Ethel Partidge gasped. "He's coming down the ramp now, see? Carrying his duffle, the lower ramp, see?"

"His woman should be meeting him," said her husband.

"Oh gaw, you mean we'll see her. Meeting her right out in open, hah? Oh, gaw, Arly, hold my hand!"

The Partidges and the Cottersley-Smiths looked after the enormous figure. They saw his hand raise suddenly, then they watched while he flagged his arm wildly. He was smiling and laughing, and it was the first time any of them could remember him doing either. But there was neither a young virginal type waiting on the wharf for Mr. Blessing, nor was there a more experienced-looking type waiting for him. In fact, a woman was not meeting Mr. Blessing at all.

Standing in the square with his legs apart and his hands on his hips—a straw hat resting back slightly on his head (as though he had pushed it back in anger or disgust) was a man. He was dressed immaculately in a white linen jacket with navy-colored linen pants, white shoes, and a red twill silk tie which was almost the same shade as his hair. Mr. Blessing was rushing toward him; a grin cut across his whole huge face, his free arm reaching out to the man. The man was alone. He did not see Mr. Blessing at first, but when he did see him, there came over his countenance one of the sourest expressions that the Arlington Partidges and the Albert Cottersley-Smiths had ever seen. It made the warm Caracas sun seem suddenly, unbelievably chilly.

Epilogue

From *The New York Daily Journal—*
WHO WAS WIN'S MURDERER?

Many people did not like Win Schneider. When the police interviewed close friends and servants of the dead woman, their list of suspects ran to two pages. There were many who might have done the deed.

Two months ago she was found strangled in the bedroom of the $99,000 home on Lerch Road in Bucks County, Pennsylvania, and the police are still trying to discover who was the one person who hated her enough to kill her. She was murdered shortly after noon on December 31, New Year's Eve day. The housekeeper was marketing in New Hope, and young Timmy Schneider was on his way to visit with his grandmother and father in New York. The Schneiders were estranged. Luther V. Schneider, President of Waverly Foods, was at his mother's house at the estimated murder-time.

There were many rumors. Talk of a fat man in a rented car being seen in the vicinity, as well as suspicions that a bitter former chauffeur had taken revenge on his ex-employer. A dazed Puerto Rican suffering from a mental illness confessed to the crime, and a brother of the murdered woman made the statement that he might have done it himself, if he had ever found time.

It was a greatly publicized case, certainly the most colorful crime in a decade.

While the murder itself was not particularly unusual, most of the people involved in the known circumstances of the case, are unusual. Luther Schneider is a millionaire. His son, Timmy, was once kidnapped and returned after Schneider paid a ransom of $100,000. The Schneider *vs* Schneider court battles still leave judges and lawyers involved in the litigation, with red ears. The murdered woman, the former Win Griswold, was a society beauty of some twenty years back. The Griswold family is well known to Eastern society circles.

WHO was Win's murderer? Who dropped the receipt near her body, the only tangible clue there is in the case, a simple piece of ordinary receipt-book paper, marked across it: PAID IN FULL?

THE END
of an Original Gold Medal Novel by
Vin Packer